{39}

The
Mysterious
Ailment

of
Rupi Baskey

A Novel

D1730360

HANSDA SOWVENDRA SHEKHAR

ALEPH

ALEPH

ALEPH BOOK COMPANY
An independent publishing firm
promoted by *Rupa Publications India*

Published in 2014 by
Aleph Book Company
7/16 Ansari Road, Daryaganj
New Delhi 110002

ISBN: 978-93-82277-32-3

1 3 5 7 9 10 8 6 4 2

Typeset in Adobe Garamond Pro by SÜRYA, New Delhi

Printed by Replika Press Pvt. Ltd., India

Marang-Buru hirla, Jaher-Ayo hirla

Bonga-Buru ar Hapram-ko lagid,
 ar Baba-Bo-Biti lagid

Contents

~

The Strongest Woman of Kadamdihi   1

Kadamdihi, Tereldihi   10

The Precious Child   22

Dular Gaatay, Reyar-Baha   45

The Groom with One Short Leg   64

The New Bride Learns New Things   73

Nitra   83

Gurubari's Wish, Rupi's Word   101

The Son with Two Mothers   106

A Whiff of Jasmine at Twilight   115

Mohni Medicine   129

The Mysterious Ailment of Rupi Baskey   143

Comparing Mysteries   149

The Wife's Revenge   159

The Fall of the Strongest Woman of Kadamdihi   165

The Next Strongest Woman of Kadamdihi   173

The Clash of the Equals   181

Alternative Therapies   186

'Is This How You Talk to Your Mother?'   197

The Cure? Well, Almost   205

Acknowledgements   209

The Strongest Woman of Kadamdihi

Rupi Baskey cannot believe she was once the strongest woman in Kadamdihi, who bore her eldest squatting in the middle of a rice paddy, shin-deep in slush.

This happened in Ashadh, in the middle of the planting season. At the time, Rupi had been in the fields with the other women, transplanting rice saplings. Her sari and petticoat were hitched up to her thigh and there were generous splashes of mud on both. Her hair had come loose over her face and, in pushing it back, she had put streaks of mud on her cheeks and forehead.

Though Rupi was not as big as she should have been at the end of a full term, her belly was quite rounded. And as she was heftily built, the duration of gestation, too, was hard to reckon. Rupi had herself been unsure, as she had never been trained in the ways of motherhood by either her mother or her mother-in-law. She only knew that she would be with child the day her husband touched her. And once she conceived, her monthly bleeding would stop. Since her knowledge was so scanty, Rupi could hardly be blamed for not knowing when she conceived. So, by the time she realized that her monthlies had ceased, the hardness in Rupi's belly had risen almost up to her navel. Then Gurubari, who had a daughter of her own, estimated that Rupi had been with child for four or five months and recommended that she visit a dhai-budhi.

'Fifth,' the midwife had declared on her very first visit.

After the dhai-budhi's declaration, Rupi had begun to count down the days to her confinement. She had not returned to Nitra—where she and Sido stayed and where he had, in all likelihood, touched her in the 'conceiving' way—but stayed on in Kadamdihi and enjoyed the benefits of being a mother-in-waiting, but only as far as her nature allowed her to do so.

~

Rupi was from Tereldihi, a village in the hills. She had grown up hunting sparrows with slingshots even as she performed the routine tasks expected of any girl in a village. She cleaned the house, washed utensils and clothes, and drew water from the well. She threw grains to the fowl and grazed the cattle and goats. She helped raise her younger siblings and cousins. She went shopping at the weekly haat in the neighbouring village of Joram, some seven kilometres from Tereldihi. Every month, she joined other girls and boys as they walked to the ration depot in Jainagar, a village at the base of the hills, and carried home bags of sugar and canisters of kerosene. In Jainagar, she attended the annual Buru-Bonga—the Worship of the Hill— held on the first Saturday of Ashadh. On some days, she visited the ancient shrine to Marang-Buru on top of the hill. She also never missed the annual Baraghat-pata. Besides all this, Rupi worked the family's fields.

After Rupi was married to Sido and brought to Kadamdihi in the plains, her life had become easier, but only just.

~

Any doctor, had she visited one, would have advised Rupi rest and proper nutrition. Food, she had in plenty. For lunch and dinner she ate rice with vegetables of all kinds: brinjal, potato,

Hansda Sowvendra Shekhar

kundri, saaru; arak-kohra made from several kinds of greens; crescents of onions, tomatoes, green chillies and salt. Occassionally, there was fish, chicken, even pigeon meat. For breakfast she ate bowls of puffed-rice khajari or beaten-rice taaben soaked in water and mixed with sugar, and a tall glass of tea.

While she had adequate nutrition, Rupi knew no rest. She had to be doing something or the other all the time. If she was not sweeping the racha, she would be cutting firewood. Or she would be boiling all the dirty quilts of the household in water and washing soda. The only pause Rupi made in her labours was a daily ritual. She would sit at a pond, scrub herself clean with a smooth, egg-shaped stone, and then wash dirty clothes with the famed Bottle-brand soap of Chakuliya.

Sido would come home from Nitra every Saturday. He would bring, along with the occasional sweets and clothes, best wishes from Bairam and Gurubari. Over the weekend he would travel to nearby villages with his younger brother, Doso, hiring labourers to work in their fields. Before leaving for Nitra, Sido would repeat to both Doso and Khorda, his father, his standing instruction to not let his pregnant wife perform any physical labour. However, once Sido left, both Khorda and Doso would forget his instruction and the entire family would collectively get down to the business of planting rice.

~

Nothing much had happened in the first two days of planting. Rupi had finished work, come home, washed, eaten, and slept like one drugged. On the third day, she had felt pain. But it had been so slight, she had ignored it. Also, she had had the dhai-budhi's assurance that she was still some time away from giving birth. She had felt contractions before, the hardening of her abdomen, but so busy did she keep herself that she had forgotten about them. But everything came rushing back when her waters broke.

She was bent over, her fingers in the mud. When she felt the warm fluid from her womb seep slowly down her thighs, she stood up, clutched at her lower back, cried loudly and toppled over into the slush. Thunder rumbled in the distance and a flock of cranes flew out of a kowha tree on the bank of the pond next to the fields. All the women working in the fields stopped what they were doing and ran to Rupi.

'Who asked her to come?' they shouted to one another.

'Sido-baahu, are you all right?' they asked her.

She yelled in agony, and the impending ordeal gave her screams power. 'Yo-go! Yo-go! Goij inan go!' Words, syllables, nonsense, she screamed whatever came to mind.

Rupi was carried to the widest aaday between two fields and laid on it. Rupi had such massive, healthy limbs that she looked like a felled banyan. The women took their time to undress her and flex her knees. When they saw that the baby's head was bobbing in and out, they quickly dispatched the men to fetch the dhai-budhi.

'It's coming!' the women shouted.

'Yo! I am dying!' Rupi shouted. Dark clouds floated ominously in the mid-June sky.

The rain waited for the baby's arrival, the baby waited for the dhai-budhi to come, and Rupi, all the while, bellowed like a cow being disembowelled alive. The women—each with three children, or four—held Rupi, implored her to have patience, and shouted at her to bear down.

'We all have to face this, baahu.'

'Keep your breaths steady. Breathe through your mouth, breathe through your mouth.'

'Push when the pain comes. Pain's coming? Pain's coming? Yes, now, push. Push!'

To all their concerned words Rupi screamed just one reply: 'Yo! I am dying!'

The dhai-budhi hobbled up, followed by Putki and Doso. Khorda, too, ran as fast as his uneven legs would allow. The women gathered in a circle around Rupi and created a shielded, makeshift labour room—the men stayed away from the scene of the birth. The dhai-budhi massaged Rupi's abdomen, inserted her fingers into the birth canal to make space for the baby's head, and egged Rupi to push with every bit of energy she possessed.

'Don't forget, baahu, this is your moment of test. You have to put your life into it. This is a very important moment for you. Don't forget, don't forget at all.'

Rupi passed the test. Jaipal was born after a few contractions and a few more words of encouragement. He was only slightly bigger than a kitten and, with his scrawny limbs, looked just like one. People sighed nervously when the dhai-budhi severed the cord and, wiping Jaipal's mouth, eyes and nostrils, held him by his legs, upside down. He first whimpered and then cried loudly. The nervous sighs turned into shrieks of delight.

'It's a boy!' the dhai-budhi cried. Khorda and Doso cheered. The rain began pelting down as Rupi was carried home on a parkom.

~

For someone who had nearly given birth on her feet, Rupi recovered quickly. In five days, she was as strong as ever, and breastfeeding tiny Jaipal whenever he demanded. She was also ready to go back to the fields.

'The planting has been completed,' Putki informed her, however.

'All of our fields?'

'Yes, baahu. You need not worry.'

~

All of this happened more than twenty years ago. Jaipal—the eldest of Rupi's three sons—is today a young man. The rift between mother and son has only widened with each passing year. This isn't the only estrangement. Over the two decades Sido, too, has moved away from her. Rupi never noticed the widening of the gap, nor did she mark when it began. How could she? Her adversary Gurubari, the one who has given her the ailment, is strong. She has sucked the life out of Rupi bit by bit and Rupi, once the strongest woman in Kadamdihi, is bedridden for no apparent reason. Her body isn't the sturdy banyan of old, it is a diseased eucalyptus: pale and covered with sickly patches.

All of Kadamdihi knows who the cause of Rupi's problem is. Gurubari, the woman who came into her life like a friend but twined around her like the alakjari—the golden vine which latches on to the trunk of a healthy, green tree, sends its roots deep into its heart and, robbing the host of all nutrition, leaves it an empty shell. It is said: Alakjari reyat muchad do okoy-e nyaam keya? It is only the most fortunate who can stop its spread. The rest can only see the vine glisten as it gains health, and the pallor which slowly spreads over the host. Just as everyone can see Rupi wasting away even as Gurubari flourishes.

~

On some days Rupi suffers a headache. On others, a funny feeling in her stomach will not let her stand or sit straight, and she has to keep lying down. Sometimes she feels such acute fatigue that she cannot walk to the pond to wash herself. She is compelled to request Dulari—Doso's wife—to fill a bucket of water for her. Rupi sits on the cot under the dogor tree and sponges herself, remembering the days when she had been compared to its fair flowers.

Sido, mostly, isn't home. He is either at work or in Gurubari's house. He sometimes travels to Ranchi to see Gurubari's daughters who live in hostels there. And even when he is home, it hardly feels like he is present. He might ask after Rupi's health, or buy her more medicines, or take her to doctors. But these are perfunctory gestures, made more out of duty than love. There is hardly any communication between man and wife.

'Don't cook anything for me,' Sido says to Rupi at times when he leaves for work. 'You are tired, you rest. I'll eat at Gurubari-hili's house.'

Or Jaipal tells her, 'Yo, I'm going with my friends to the pata. If I'm late I'll spend the night at Gurubari-marak-ayo's house. Don't wait up for me.'

These words, hili and marak-ayo, burn her up: hili, the wife of one's elder brother; marak-ayo, the wife of the elder brother of one's father. Had Gurubari been a good woman, Rupi would have never objected to her man and children having anything to do with her. But she knows—as does everyone—that Gurubari has gone beyond being a mere hili to Sido. Rupi has seen this for herself in Nitra. Further, Rupi hears rumours that Gurubari is Sido's keep. Worse than those are the stories that Sido has become Gurubari's. And even though all ties of kinship have now become hollow, and though Rupi is desperate to protest the hold Gurubari has on her family, she cannot. For every time she tries, she is overcome by an insurmountable enervation.

~

Rupi is the last person in the world to find out that Jaipal, her firstborn, is contemplating marriage. The fact hurts, and though she is quick to realize that times have changed and she is not a strong woman any more, tears flood her eyes.

Helplessness, regret and anger race across her face. Helplessness—for things are entirely out of her control. Regret—at having been so careless. Anger—at herself and at others. She hates Putki because she drinks too much and hawks stories about her own family to everyone; she hates Gurubari and she hates Dulari, for both know dahni-bidya. Rupi is filled with anger for everyone. She looks up at the dogor leaves and in spite of herself, as if it were a crime to cry, permits the tears to roll down her cheeks.

Putki watches her daughter-in-law weep and regrets telling her about Jaipal. She craves another glass of home-brewed haandi and blissful, sound sleep. This is what the many decades of her life have taught her: drink, throw all worries to the wind and live life to the fullest. She thinks of Della, her Reyar-Baha, her beloved Winter Flower. Putki reflects on her miserable present and feels Della's comforting closeness around her. Sorrow engulfs her, as does the overpowering thirst for another baati of haandi.

'Go!' Dulari taunts. 'Your friends must be waiting for you. They will give you haandi in a bigger baati today.'

'You dahni!' Putki screeches. 'Eat me, come! Eat me. Finish me up today. What is stopping you? Then you'll never see me go out for another drop of haandi.'

'I'll leave that to your elder son's hirom,' Dulari says through clenched teeth, the witch inside her enranged by the provocation, her eyes red, her breath heavy. 'To that Gurubari. She's doing a better job than I can. Why should I intervene? Rupi-dai is half dead already. And you are already on your way to the gada-dharay.'

'You dahni!' Putki screams. 'You'll finish us all. You'll…'

Dulari turns away, smirking. Putki is sure that Rupi has heard this exchange. She knows that Rupi is crying. She is convinced that this is her punishment for being a bad woman and a bad mother. What the people of Kadamdihi say is true; the immorality of Putki's youth has come back to haunt her. Rupi's disease isn't hers alone. It is Putki's, it is Sido's, Doso's and Dulari's. It will perhaps finish them all, their entire family.

Their house has become a spectacle. It has always been one— from the time Putki flitted from man to man to the day Rupi bore Jaipal in a rice paddy, to the day Sido chose Gurubari and Dulari slew Doso's lover. Each episode in their lives has played out in full view of Kadamdihi, even as the village has speculated about them, cheered them on, lamented their fate and, most of all, enjoyed the show.

Kadamdihi, Tereldihi

Kadamdihi was named after the kadam tree. No kadam trees are to be found in Kadamdihi anymore, but Putki recalls that there were many when her father, the formidable Somai-haram, and other elders founded the village.

'There was a forest of kadam trees down by the stream, my father used to say,' Putki announces over a baati of haandi at the house of the majhi where she usually drinks.

Somai-haram is long dead, as are the friends of his youth. However, there is no disputing Putki's claim or her father's authority. If Somai-haram claimed to have seen kadam trees in Kadamdihi, then there must have been kadam trees in the village.

'If that man was so good,' a young bride of the majhi's house, new to the village, asks her mother-in-law, 'why is this woman in such a state?'

'What do you think happens to a haandi-togoij-maiju?' her mother-in-law, a sage lady who has seen Putki at her wildest, whispers. 'All her life she has lived with no care, only drinking and changing men. What other fate can befall such a woman?'

'But her sons? What did they do? Sido is an educated man, after all.'

'Education is of no use if one lacks common sense. Who asked him to carry on with that Gurubari? She was nicely married to that Bairam-mastar, and Sido had found such a good wife in Rupi. Now everyone's life is spoilt. Sido's, Rupi's, everyone's. Except that Gurubari's. As for Doso, he was a wild bull. What Dulari has done to him is very good. He deserves it.'

As the young bride nods her head, a raspy, quavering voice rises. The bride freezes. It is only when the other women of the house start laughing that she realizes that the voice belongs to Putki who, in her drunken stupor, has decided to tell the story of Kadamdihi through song.

Aalay bargay ray ma, kocha bargay ray ma
Kadam mulin baha poroi-poroi

In our garden, our corner garden
Look! The kadam flowers have blossomed

Putki ululates the song, her eyes drowsy, her face an impassive, craggy sheet of wax. Her shrivelled breasts droop out of her sari. Putki once used to wear blouses but, as she grew older, she began dressing like the other women of the village; in a sari wound around the waist and then around the torso, without a petticoat or a blouse. When Rupi had been healthy, she had always made sure that Putki was adequately covered. But now, Putki has gone back to her slatternly ways.

Putki waves her hands in tune with her song. 'This song,' Putki tells her hosts, 'Della used to sing this song. My friend Della, you remember her, don't you?'

They do. Della, Putki's soulmate, her partner-in-crime. The stories of their escapades are always deliciously titillating, which was why the women of the house of the majhi liked to host Putki.

'We heard this song in a gaayaan in Chakuliya. It was a long time ago, a long time ago. Both of us were working at the rice mill then.'

Though the women have heard the story many times, they enjoy each telling of it. So they listen in rapt attention as Putki recalls each event as if it happened only yesterday.

She begins quite matter-of-factly: 'Two men were lusting after Della then.' But all the women gathered around smile and blush. 'They followed us into the tent. Della and I held on to each other and laughed.' Putki laughs. Some haandi spills and she nearly chokes on her drink.

'Careful, Putki-jhi!' Someone steps forward to help the old lady. Putki laughs some more, and spills more haandi. The older women of the house shuffle nervously, expecting a mishap. With Putki, no one can be sure.

And accident there is, right under the gaando on which Putki sits! A yellow stream flows towards the audience and Putki is completely unaware of it.

'Haaye Chando!' the mother-in-law screams. 'What has this woman done?'

The women, all of whom know Putki and her ways quite well, laugh. One exclaims, 'This is what happens when you drink so much. All of us drink, but we don't go around pissing everywhere. Putki drinks like a man!'

Somai-haram's daughter looks around, bleary-eyed, at the commotion around her, shakes her head and leans against the wall. She is soon asleep and snoring, her sari soaked in haandi and piss.

The oldest woman of the majhi's house, well above ninety years, muses wistfully, 'Her father was a good man. How did this girl turn out this way?'

~

Kadamdihi lies north of Chakuliya, which is the nearest big town and railhead from Kadamdihi. Some forty kilometres to the west of Chakuliya, along the rail route, is Ghatshila. Further on from Ghatshila is Jamshedpur, the steel city. Dhalbhumgarh, the seat of the Dhal kings who once ruled the area, falls almost exactly between Chakuliya and Ghatshila. Forty kilometres to the east of Chakuliya is Jhargram, in the state of West Bengal; while Baharagora lies forty kilometres to the south of Chakuliya. This entire area—Chakuliya, Kadamdihi, Ghatshila, Dhalbhumgarh, Baharagora and other neighbouring villages— is on the lowermost tip of Jharkhand and is wedged between West Bengal and Odisha.

The paaris, or surname, of Somai-haram's gushti is Hansda. The eldest male of this clan was chosen as the majhi of Kadamdihi and his house occupied prime position at the top of its main street. The other people who make up Santhali society were chosen from the rest of the Santhal families in the village. This included the naikay—the bridge between the residents of the village and their gods—whose house was opposite Somai-haram's. The paaris of the naikay-gushti is Marndi. The jogmajhi—the organizer of weddings and funerals, as well as the meetings of the moray-ko, the five village elders, also found a plot at the head of the kulhi. The gushti of the jogmajhi bears the paaris Murmu. The godeth, the village crier, had a house at the end of the kulhi where the Kamar lived. The gushti of the godeth bears the paaris Tudu. Tudu men are also called Tudu-kora-rusika. They are considered to be lovers of poetry, music and the arts. Because of their love for the finer things of life, Tudu men are said to impress women easily and it is considered to be a disgrace for a Tudu man to not be involved with more than one woman at the same time.

Each paaris has its own story about how it came into being. Hansdas, for instance, are said to have hatched from the eggs of the mythical swans, Hans and Hansli, while Murmus are believed to be the kids of the the sacred nanny-goat, Murum-Enga. Since all Hansdas are considered to be fellow nestlings, a Hansda man can never marry a Hansda woman. And so it is with others. Further, a marriage may take place between a man and a woman from the same village if they aren't related by blood and bear different surnames; but since a village, too, is seen as an extended family, a marriage within one's village is often looked down upon.

In time, two other communities arrived in Kadamdihi. They were the Kamar: the blacksmiths, and the Kunkal: the potters. Two kulhis branched out from the main kulhi of Kadamdihi on two different sides. The Kamars took one and the Kunkals took the other.

The Kamar and the Kunkal are Hindu and worship the idols of their gods, unlike the Santhals who follow the Sarna religion and worship nature and its spirits. The Kamar and the Kunkal belong to the lower rungs of the caste ladder of the Hindu religion. But both used to consider the Santhals of Kadamdihi impure and uncivilized as they ate cow and pig meat, drank haandi and paura, and practised polygamy. They kept a close eye on their things if a Santhal happened to venture into their kulhis, for they believed that even the shadow of a Santhal was enough to defile them. If Santhal children played on their properties, they made sure to remind them to not touch their things or animals, accidentally or otherwise, for it would contaminate them all. Furthermore, no Kamar or Kunkal would eat or even drink water in the presence of a Santhal or in a Santhal house.

The Santhals stayed quiet, attended to their own businesses and never raised their voice against such discrimination, content that Kadamdihi was, ultimately, a Santhal village. On one occasion, though, the simmering anger boiled over.

~

Sido was a bright child, and among the few Santhal boys from Kadamdihi to attend school. The other students in his school belonged mostly to the Mahato and Maarh communities from neighbouring villages. Both the Mahatos and the Maarhs are relatively prosperous, landowning communities and are above the Kamars and the Kunkals in the caste heirarchy. There's a popular saying which indicates how the Maarhs are commonly perceived: 'Maarh gyalo gorob-e, Saotal gyalo porob-e'. Arrogance is the undoing of the Maarhs while merrymaking is the undoing of the Santhals.

As for the Mahatos, they are the subjects of several jokes. There is one about a Mahato man who went to his in-laws' place for the first time after marriage. He was seated next to his father-in-law and, unsure how to strike up a conversation with the old man, asked him, quite stupidly, if he was married. 'Ki baw, sosur, byiha korinchho?'

Jokes about Mahatos might make them look stupid. However, they are extremely hard-working and shrewd people with a propensity for thrift and a knack for survival. They can smell out their own even in a crowd of a million and stick to others of their community in times of crisis. If one were to compare Santhals and Mahatos, it would be concluded that a Santhal, despite his riches, may die of hunger, but a Mahato, however poor, will never starve.

Sido was in high school at that time, a boy of thirteen or fourteen. Once, while herding his goats away from a Kamar's garden, he accidentally brushed against the Kamar woman who had been working there.

The woman got up bawling. 'Ei Saotal chhana-ta amake chhui dilo! Hey bhogobaan!' She then ranted at length about having been made impure.

Sido was furious. He got up, dusted his knees, and herded his goats into the garden. 'Kaati de na, go, chamra-ta!' he screamed. 'Did I touch your hand? Here, let me touch it again. Then you can cut it off as well.' He advanced menacingly towards the woman, brandishing the bamboo cane he carried. She fled.

Later, an indirect complaint was made to Khorda-haram. As Kadamdihi was a Santhal village, all grievances had to be put up before the majhi. Untouchability was an issue that concerned the non-Santhals alone, so such a misdemeanour could hardly be brought up before the majhi. The most that the Kamars could do was to shout at the top of their voices from their own kulhis. The shouting, in Sido's case, was louder because he, unlike other Santhal children, had not shrunk back and tolerated discrimination but, instead, faced down the woman.

'Look what that Saotal kid did to me,' the Kamar woman screamed. 'That Sido, that lame Khorda's son. That Sido, he threatened to touch me with his hands, his dirty hands. Doesn't he know we are clean people? These Saotal, these cow-eating, pig-eating, dirty Saotal, they know nothing about us, about our religion. They will pollute us. We must not tolerate this any more.'

Other Kamars joined in. Men, women, all. 'Yes, these dirty, cow-eating Saotal, they understand nothing. How hard we try to preserve our faith, our position, what do they know? Such acts will not be tolerated any more.'

This had gone too far. The Santhals had given too much freedom to non-Santhals in their own village. All the men gathered before Putki's house, each with a long wooden staff, and marched together to the Kamar-kulhi. This small army had only reached the head of the Kamar-kulhi when they were noticed by the Kamar men and women. The screaming stopped. Within seconds the Kamar-kulhi cleared and the street became as silent as a crematorium at midnight. The doors were bolted shut, windows were closed, women dragged their bawling children into their houses and slapped them till they became quiet. There was not even a dog or a chicken to be seen.

Some of the Santhal men laughed. One of them said, 'They don't have the nerve to face us and yet they dare to tell us who is clean and who is unclean.' They then marched into the Kamar-kulhi.

Khorda-haram spoke in his loudest voice. 'Listen, all of you. All of you who are not a part of us Saotal. When you all came seeking a home in this village, this village that we Saotal built, our fathers and uncles never refused you. They took you in like brothers and expected all of you to live thus. This did not happen. We Saotal men, women and children leave no stone unturned to maintain harmony. We remain silent despite your discrimination. You call our children dirty when they play in your fields, but you happily walk into ours and shit in them. Do we chase you out? You move your clothes and baskets out of our way when we walk on your street, as if we suffer from some contagious disease. Today, my son accidentally touched one of you and all of you started shouting as if he has committed a crime. If my son committed a crime, then your woman, too, committed a crime by coming in my son's way. We may all be dirty, but how clean are you? If we brushed your clothes, we'd end up with so much dirt, it would make a statue the size of a man. That is how dirty you all are! Your mouths smell worse than our backsides. That is how dirty you all are! Yes, we eat cow and pig meat, but our minds are cleaner than yours. We know how to live in peace. And we know what to do with people who don't let us live in peace. Let what has happened today never be repeated. We are the ones who have let you live in this village; we can very well force you to pack up and leave. One word more against our women, children and religion, and see what happens to you all. Don't forget.'

Khorda-haram, who had never spoken one straight sentence in the rustic Bangla the Kamar spoke, was so charged with emotion that he made his speech without hesitation, without stammering. That his speech was full of inaccuracies—of language and pronunciation, even in that crude dialect—was quite evident. On any other day, his speech would have had people rolling around with laughter.

Khorda-haram was a guileless, simple man who believed in making others happy and loved to see people smiling and at peace. But on that day, he was different. It wasn't as if only his son had been accused, his entire community had been blamed.

The speech worked. From then on, not a word was spoken by the non-Santhals against Santhals. Publicly, at least.

~

Khorda-haram was known to be a man of principle. Somai-haram, his father-in-law, was revered even after his death. Sido was well known outside of Kadamdihi because of his grandfather and father, and also because he was educated, and already a teacher. Thus, it was but natural for Rupi's family in Tereldihi to be overwhelmed with joy and surprise when they came to know that Khorda was considering their daughter for marriage with his son.

Tereldihi, too, was named after a tree—the terel or the kendu whose leaves are used to roll bidis with. It is a small village on the border of Jharkhand and West Bengal, a little way off the road that comes from Chakuliya, passes Kadamdihi, Joram and Jainagar and enters West Bengal. Unlike Kadamdihi, which was more cosmopolitan because of the three different communities which lived there and its proximity to Chakuliya, Tereldihi was a wholly Santhal village. And because it was located inside a forest, the village was quite remote. Chakuliya was too far away for the people of Tereldihi and they visited the town only for important work. For instance, to catch a train, or if they had something to do at the block office, or if they worked at one of the mills in Chakuliya.

For business, such as selling firewood, terel leaves and matkom blossoms, and to buy the things they needed, the villagers of Tereldihi crossed over to Belpahari in West Bengal, a village only a little smaller than Chakuliya.

Till she married Sido, Rupi could count her visits to Chakuliya on the fingers of her hands. The journeys had all been made in bullock carts, together with other members of the family. The cluster of trees outside Kadamdihi had always drawn her attention.

'Yo, which place is this?' she asked her mother on one of their journeys.

'This is Kadamdihi,' one of the aunts who were accompanying her, said, adding, 'See how she asks every time which place this is? As if she doesn't know.'

'How would I know?' Rupi said, taken aback by the sharpness of her aunt's tone. 'I don't travel to these places often.'

'Weren't you told the last time?' another aunt asked.

'Yes,' Rupi said. 'But I forgot.'

'Don't forget one thing,' the first aunt said mischievously. 'There are very rich farmers living in Kadamdihi. One day, we will get you married off to one.'

Rupi blushed like a joba-kusum in full bloom.

'Why any man?' Rupi's mother said on her behalf. 'We will marry her to the son of the majhi of Kadamdihi.'

'The majhi's sons are already married,' the second aunt pointed out.

'So what? There must be at least one unmarried young man in the majhi-gushti. We will get our Rupi married to him.'

For the rest of the journey, Rupi remained doubled up in shyness like a pangolin.

There were no kadam trees in Kadamdihi, but Tereldihi was surrounded by a forest that not only had terel but also sarjom, matkom, kowha, tarop, bhurru, mango and jackfruit trees. In fact, the forest one had to cross to reach Tereldihi was so dense, many felt it had been sheer arrogance on Khorda-haram's part to reject all suitable girls from the plains and choose someone from the hills for his son. But they took one look at Rupi and all doubts went scuttling out of their minds. She was pretty, submissive in the way all brides ought to be and, being a Hembram girl who did not share her prospective husband's surname, belonged to the right paaris. She couldn't read a single letter in either of the Roman, Devanagari, Bangla or Ol-Chiki scripts, but her virtues weighed far heavier than this minor shortcoming of hers. She was tall, healthy, strong-limbed, and her complexion was lighter than that of the other girls Khorda-haram had seen.

'Yes,' he had declared. 'I choose her for my son.'

The rancour at missing the opportunity to be married to Khorda-haram's son had been strong. This resentment became keener when people recalled that Khorda-haram's own wife, Putki, had been no angel herself. In fact, the marriage between Khorda and Putki had been viewed by many as a marriage of convenience. Khorda was a widower, and Putki had had relationships before marriage. Many had even pointed out that the marriage was a solution devised by Somai-haram to keep his wayward daughter in check.

~

The people of Kadamdihi are certain that the collective curses of all the families whose daughters Khorda-haram rejected

Hansda Sowvendra Shekhar

brought misery into Putki's life. They still remember how happily the bariyat had walked all the way to Tereldihi. The camaraderie between the two brothers, Sido and Doso, had been worth witnessing. Sido couldn't have known at that time that his wedding would be the last proper wedding in their family for a long while—with a bariyat and the excitement of bringing home a bride—and that they would have to wait for Bishu's turn to see a proper wedding. The smile on Khordaharam's lips had revealed what he was feeling inside: absolute elation. For once, it had seemed as if Putki, despite having wasted a good portion of her youth, had finally found happiness and peace with a good husband and two capable sons.

The villagers sigh. 'Who is to blame?' someone says. 'Putki was never meant to be miserable. She'd have lived like a queen. But then...'

The Precious Child

Putki was a precious child, born to Somai-haram's first wife, Older Somai-budhi, after she had miscarried three times.

The first miscarriage happened in the dead of the night, in the second month of pregnancy, when even Older Somai-budhi hadn't been sure of the changes taking place in her body.

At the time of the abortion, Somai-haram and his first wife had been married for more than ten years—eleven, twelve, perhaps; even they themselves couldn't say for sure. They had occassionally contemplated adoption, for Somai-haram wouldn't bring home a second wife. Somai-haram had brothers and cousins all over Kadamdihi and its sprawling majhi-gushti. They could have asked anyone for a child. Somehow, though, they had managed to keep their contemplation to themselves for more than a decade, discussing it only over dinner when Somai-haram ate and Older Somai-budhi looked on. Or when they lay down to sleep but were too tired to drift easily into slumber. Their childlessness chafed, then, and made them so sore that they had to speak about it.

'How many days more before this life will end?' Older Somai-budhi asked, each word of her question heavy with the stigma of barrenness which no one mentioned directly to her, but which must have been a recurring topic of conversation in almost each house of the village, whether Santhal or Kamar or Kunkal.

'Life is very long; we have many more years to live,' Somai-haram said. He was conscious of the hollowness of his words but couldn't help it; he had to cheer up his wife. Barrenness was a tremendous burden to bear, he understood very well. And to add to it was the constant pressure he was under to either remarry or to adopt a child. With the kind of farm he had and the rice crops he raised, anyone would jump at the prospect of becoming his successor. After the majhi, Somai-haram deposited the largest quantity of rice with the raja of Dhalbhumgarh. Somai-haram made sure that he never discussed adoption openly, he never raised the topic in public, and he had also instructed Older Somai-budhi quite strictly to not lament her childlessness before all and sundry. 'We will have a child,' he assured her. But he would consider his greying hair, his age, and the occasional weariness he felt. He would think: Will I be able to have a child? When?

Somai-haram soon received answers. But the proof of his virility was just a few lumps of bloody tissue Older Somai-budhi expelled from her womb in her sleep.

'This doesn't matter,' Somai-haram said to reassure his wife. His disappointment at losing the foetus was lessened by the glorious revelation that he could still sire offspring.

Older Somai-budhi's mother also visited. 'Next time, mai,' she said. 'Don't be sad.'

In the commiseration that followed her miscarriage, Older Somai-budhi forgot to mention to anyone the dream that she had had on the night the tissue from her womb flowed out in a bloody, mucoid gush. She had seen a large woman whose hair was open and flying wildly like pennants in a strong wind. She saw that, and the woman's big eyes which did not stop rolling. Left right up down, left right up down—they moved like two glass marbles placed on a plate. She couldn't see her face. And though she had later asked herself how she could see—and remember so well—the woman's eyes but not her face, she had not felt that the matter was important enough to discuss with either her mother or her husband. It was just a dream, she thought, it couldn't have been connected with her miscarriage.

The second stillborn foetus arrived in the fifth month of pregnancy, in a gush of dirty water. Its body was so scrawny and pale that it looked like a plucked chicken. Somai-haram and other men buried the foetus before telling Older Somai-budhi about her dead child. By the time they reached her bedside, she knew that the birth had been premature, that the baby was dead and that it had most likely already been buried in a corner of the property marked as a crematorium for members of Somai-haram's family. She had braced herself for unpleasant news. Yet when the dhai-budhi whispered into her ear, 'Jeevee ketej taam, baahu,' Older Somai-budhi had felt the pain inside her womb drift away with the large teardrops that rolled in a silent, continuous stream from her eyes. After those words she heard nothing more. Older Somai-budhi gave in to the fatigue of parturition and drifted off into a deep, undisturbed sleep.

The routine of Older Somai-budhi's life was disturbed after a few years when she discovered that she was pregnant again. She was much older now and Somai-haram had greyed considerably, but their desire for a child had remained undiminished.

They had been trying, Somai-haram and his wife, but conception hadn't been easy. Somai-haram, the devout Sarna that he was, and a member of the majhi-gushti, had regularly prayed to the deities. He went to the Kadamdihi stream everyday for his morning bath. Afterwards, he would wash his clothes, change into a fresh dhoti and, on his way back home, stop at the jaher to kneel before the shrine of Marang-Buru and his consort Jaher-Ayo.

~

The shrine of Marang-Buru and Jaher-Ayo is the holiest spot in the jaher, the place where the sacrifices are made during Baha—the spring festival—and Maak-Moray. It is at the jaher that the gods ascend the bodies of mediums. The mediums are all men and even Jaher-Ayo, a female deity, climbs on to the body of a man. Amongst Santhals, women's bodies are not considered appropriate vessels to receive gods. In some villages, the Baha and Maak-Moray festivals are held on the same day in the month of Fagun. In others, Baha is held first, in Fagun, while Maak-Moray is held at a later date, chosen by each village according to its convenience. During Baha, chickens are sacrificed, while goats are offered during Maak-Moray. The meat of all sacrificed animals is cooked and distributed among the residents of the village.

The shrine of Marang-Buru and Jaher-Ayo was set up under a canopy of hay tied on to a bamboo frame and supported by four bamboo sticks. The shrine was surrounded by four tall sarjom trees—the sarjom is sacred to the followers of Sarna. Somai-haram knelt before this shrine first, touched his head to the ground and mumbled prayers at length, patiently explaining his needs to the most revered couple of the Sarna pantheon—the Father and the Mother. He reminded them of the good deeds that he had performed; he reminded them that he had been a faithful servant to all the gods, and that he had observed all customs faithfully. After this, he rose and circumambulated the jaher, bowing at the four other shrines.

There were five more shrines at the jaher besides the shrine of Marang-Buru and Jaher-Ayo. To the right of Marang-Buru and Jaher-Ayo stood the shrine of feminine power, of fertility. On the left stood the Five Great Warriors, the Moray-Ko. The shrine further left of the shrine of Moray-Ko was the shrine of Sendra-Ko—the Hunters, the shrine of masculine power. In front of Marang-Buru and Jaher-Ayo was the shrine of Dharma. These four shrines were marked by a bamboo stick fixed in the earth and a mound built up at the base of each. Every year during Baha, the bamboo at each shrine would be topped by a fresh cone of hay. The shrine of the Moray-Ko could be identified by the remnants of clay figurines of haathi and saadom—elephants and horses—which were offered every year. The figurines, which were not periodically cleared away, were heaped in a pile.

The fifth shrine, set apart from the others, was devoid of offerings and embellishments. It did not even have a bamboo stick or a mound to mark it as a shrine. There was only a plain patch of earth, more than a foot wide, which had been smoothened by use year after year. There was some grass growing on this patch of earth. Each year, during Baha and Maak-Moray, this smooth patch of earth would be shorn of grass and polished with cow dung. The naikay would then draw squares with grains of arwa rice after which a black chicken would be sacrificed and buried whole near the shrine. Then the naikay would bow down to offer prayers. No one other than the naikay knelt before Sima-Bonga, the deity of this mysterious, isolated shrine.

While the other gods represent positive energy, Sima-Bonga symbolizes the negative forces. It causes disease, infirmity, poverty, doom and, finally, death. In order to keep the village safe from its evil influence, Sima-Bonga, too, must be paid obeisance along with the other deities. And though Sima-Bonga is worshipped only during the Baha and Maak-Moray festivals, and no one prays to it on ordinary days, there are people who tame it. For these people, Sima-Bonga takes precedence even over the Father and the Mother or over Karam-Bonga, the deity who looks after families.

Sima-Bonga is said to bring easy wealth to those who appease it. Hence, it is also called the Dhonkundra-bhoot. It manifests itself as a small child—or a dwarf, no taller than three feet—with large, saucer-like eyes and a small, pinched mouth. White from head to toe, it comes out to play in the night. It jumps from one baandi to the other in the granaries of rich men, singing:

Nowa do aleyak baandi
Nowa ho aleyak baandi
Nowa do Kaalay-ak baandi

This is our baandi
This, too, is our baandi
This one is Kaalay's baandi

However, the Dhonkundra-bhoot extracts a heavy price for its favours. People who maintain it usually suffer strange, incurable illnesses. Some of them—both men and women, but more men than women—become sterile and never sire or bear children. And the children they do have turn out to be weaklings or imbeciles. Also, there is the shrill, annoying, almost maddening cry of the Dhonkundra-bhoot which its tamer must endure. 'E-ba! E-ba!' the bhoot cries out to its master. 'E-yo! E-yo!' it cries out to the master's wife. These ululations are painful, like those of a child's whose fingers have been trapped in the hinges of a door. It is said that those who appease this bhoot hear its cries all the time and eventually lose their minds. Yet, the lure of easy wealth compels people to tame Sima-Bonga.

When Somai-haram paid obeisance at the jaher, he bowed before each shrine. However, he just regarded Sima-Bonga from afar. It was a perfunctory gesture, so that it couldn't accuse him of neglect. He wanted a child; he did not want Older Somai-budhi to miscarry yet again.

~

The prospect of motherhood excited Older Somai-budhi. She invited her mother over when, at the end of the fourth month, she felt the baby move inside her. Older Somai-budhi's mother had stayed with her daughter for just over a week, helping her with household chores—cooking, chopping firewood, sweeping the house—when Older Somai-budhi realized that the child had stopped kicking.

'There's nothing to worry about,' her mother said. 'Babies don't kick all the time.'

Older Somai-budhi tried to relax, she tried to keep her mind occupied, but it was difficult. The pain of her last miscarriage and the long wait made her impatient. Two entire days passed by with the baby immobile and with Older Somai-budhi in agonized suspense.

Her mother tried to soothe Older Somai-budhi. 'See, is anything untoward happening to you? Anything? Anything at all? You would've known. Nothing is wrong, mai, nothing is wrong. You are worrying for nothing.'

Older Somai-budhi was distressed. 'No, yo,' she insisted, 'something is happening. I can feel it.'

Something was indeed happening. Two days later, Older Somai-budhi passed a few clots the size of her fist when she squatted in the space behind the house, under the dogor tree, to relieve herself. Panicked, she rose and her loins began to ache. She somehow managed to drag herself to the back door.

'Yo! Yo!' she screamed in agony and in shock. 'It's happening, yo. I told you, yo. It's happening!'

Older Somai-budhi's mother found her squatting outside the

Hansda Sowvendra Shekhar

door, propped against the wall for strength and support, sobbing hysterically. Her sari and petticoat were hitched up and stained with blood and thick, brownish fluid. Between her feet was a lump—the dead foetus dangled from Older Somai-budhi's body by its umbilical cord.

~

Older Somai-budhi's mother had always harboured doubts. And when her daughter told her of the dream she had had all those years ago, during her first pregnancy, her fears were nearly confirmed. She knew of a huge woman who lived in the house which faced Somai-haram's house. She was the naikay's wife.

'I shall talk to your husband about this,' Older Somai-budhi's mother said to her. 'This is a serious matter. You will lose all your children this way. And you know as well as I do that you're not getting any younger. And nor is jawai.'

'Are you sure he will listen to you?'

'That, you should know better than I. But why won't he? He's losing his children. He should listen.'

And so it was decided. Older Somai-budhi's mother would voice her doubts and talk about the safety of her daughter and the children that she would—if ever—carry in future. The only problem was that this was a very sensitive issue. Older Somai-budhi's mother, an outsider, would be casting aspersions on the people of Kadamdihi. That, Somai-haram might find offensive.

'Jawai,' she began, 'why do you think this is happening to my daughter?' She then went on to tell Somai-haram about his wife's dream and their speculation about the identity of the woman in it.

As Older Somai-budhi's mother had feared, Somai-haram ignored the real issue at hand and instead took offence at the implications of what she was saying. 'What do you want to say, yo?' he asked. 'Do you mean that it is the naikay's wife who is behind the deaths of my children?'

Older Somai-budhi's mother gauged her son-in-law's rising temper and softened her stance. 'I don't blame her. But you surely must have heard stories about her.'

'That is not for you to tell me. Don't judge the people of my village; take stock of what is happening in yours.'

Somai-haram refused to speak to his mother-in-law any further on this issue and, slighted thus, Older Somai-budhi's mother set out for her village early the very next morning. She informed her daughter and son-in-law about her leaving the night before because she did not want the elaborate formalities of departure to be observed. The conversation with her son-in-law had disappointed her deeply, and she did not want to stay in Kadamdihi for even one extra minute.

Somai-haram was offended by his mother-in-law's hinting that the naikay's wife might be responsible for his wife's miscarriages, but a part of him was convinced that her fears could have basis in fact.

He thought of his wife and her dream. A huge woman with long hair and big, rolling eyes. Why, that was the naikay's wife. The naikay's wife was much younger than Somai-haram, perhaps younger than Older Somai-budhi, too. But since Somai-haram addressed the naikay—a frail old man with a face like an ape— as dada, elder brother, he had to call the naikay's wife hili.

The naikay's wife was a tall, dark woman with strong limbs and long hair whose will reigned supreme in her household. She kept herself and her house immaculate, she could work as well and as hard as three men put together, and she hated people who loitered about or wasted time. She had a voice which could fell trees and her singing was like the rumbling of clouds. Occasionally, she would get drunk on haandi and remember the songs of her youth.

Haram kaadaa-y thaali a-kan
Gidhi maylay-maylay
Kiya baha mohay a-kan
Kora maylay-maylay

The old he-buffalo is caught in the mire
Greedy vultures eye him, their mouths water
The young woman has bloomed like the fragrant kiya flower
Young men lust after her, their mouths water

Whenever the mischief of the children of the village angered her, she would raise her fist and shout, 'Emon kilan kilabo panjra dhilabo!' It was a treat to watch this hill of a woman stand in the middle of the kulhi shouting in her reverberating baritone. The children would flee at the sight while the men and women would laugh. The adults of the village understood that the naikay's wife wasn't seriously thinking of striking the errant children so hard that their very ribcages would crack, but they knew enough of her to be afraid.

The adults of Kadamdihi would discuss the strange and frightening happenings of their village in the safe confines of their houses—the mysterious death of a man; the unexplained deaths of the majhi's calves; and Older Somai-budhi's three consecutive miscarriages. They would whisper to one another.

'Is the naikay's wife to blame?'

'Someone saw her by the stream that night, with some other women.'

'All of them dahnis!'

'Wasn't the naikay's wife hovering around the majhi's byre that night? The guti-ko saw her, they said.'

Somai-haram did not know for how long his mother-in-law, a wise woman herself, had lived with her doubt. She must have wanted to talk about it with him. Perhaps, but how could she?

How could she expect Somai-haram to break the harmony which existed in Kadamdihi and look with suspicion at a woman he treated as a sister-in-law? So many women possessed the skill, the knowledge of the dark practices. It could've been anyone, and not necessarily the naikay's wife. Anyone? Who? This bothered Somai-haram now. So many women—Santhal, Kamar, Kunkal, Mahato—possessed the knowledge. How could he pin the blame on just one?

Despite her reputation, of which everyone spoke in hushed voices, the naikay's wife was the life of every gathering. Her mesmerizing, maternal smile concealed the power which came over her on certain nights. This power which knew no difference of gender, caste, religion, community or village. On ordinary days, when the naikay's wife was mock-threatening the village children or singing drunkenly, she'd be an ordinary Santhal woman, a follower of Sarna, untouchable to most Kamar and Kunkal women. But when the dahnis gathered on certain konami nights, all barriers of religions and prejudices of community would be forgotten. They would meet in the bamboo thicket outside the village, roam the banks of the Kadamdihi stream, ritually suck the life out of humans and animals and, in the absence of prey, devour human or animal dung. They would conjure up balls of fire the size of rice pots, host the Bhaatu—their master, their sacred tiger—comb the Bhaatu's fur, plan sacrifices, carry them out, and dance the euphoric dance of oneness with their power. Somai-haram had received reports of these gatherings from time to time.

~

Two Kamar men were on their way home after visiting relatives in another village. This village was quite far away and it had taken them half a day to walk there and half to return. It was around ten in the night when they reached the outer border of Kadamdihi: the stream which was quite close to the Santhals's jaher. It was a konami night, there were no clouds in the sky, the calmness of the hour extended over the brightly lit landscape and into the distance.

The track before them was clear and they walked fast. They had been out earlier on several occasions, they had even been delayed, but this night was different. It carried within it a strange fear. Those were the days of peculiar beings, of creatures which emerged after dark: apparition horses; boars which materialized out of thin air and mauled anyone who was unfortunate enough to cross their paths; pale, childlike beings which sat in bushes on the sides of roads and stared at passers-by with their saucer-like eyes; women who fed on the hearts and livers of men, women and children. With these fears bubbling inside them, they hurried on as noiselessly as possible.

The village lay silent before them. A few strides more and they would be home. From the bank of the Kadamdihi stream they could see that the main street on the other side was deserted. The villagers slept early, at eight or nine. Evenings in Kadamdihi were illuminated by harkane lanterns and dibas, and before going to bed, the villagers would snuff out every flame.

The two men raised their lungis above their knees and waded into the stream. The stones were slippery and one wrong step could injure, or worse, delay them.

Shappal... Shappal... Shappal... They waded across, trying to make as little noise as possible. Tall bigna and omori shrubs on both sides of the stream obscured their vision. Anyone could be hiding behind those plants and they wouldn't know. Kadamdihi wasn't known for its thieves and robbers, nor were the villages nearby. Bandits and robbers of the Lodha community lived in the forests but they hardly made their way into the villages, unless they planned some big heist. The only things to fear were the supernatural horses, the angry boars and the bloodthirsty women. Shappal… Shappal… Shappal… One man waded through and had nearly emerged on to the bank. 'Done,' he sighed in relief, and turned around. He was shocked to see his companion still in midstream.

'Hey!' he whispered, panicky. 'What are you doing? Walk faster!'

The other man stared fixedly at a part of the distant bank of the stream which was quite concealed by omori shrubs.

'What? What are you looking at?' the man near the bank whispered furiously.

The other man bobbed his head towards the bank.

The other man looked in the direction indicated and froze.

Four women gambolled naked, their bodies illuminated by moonlight, unmindful of being out in the open, utterly unconcerned about who was watching them. Every now and then, they reached down to pick something off the grass and put it in their mouths. Energized by their snack, they resumed walking. Their heads bobbed to some inaudible beat—right left right left right left.

The Kamar men felt their legs turn to stone. The water in the stream seemed to turn to ice and they stood frozen, unsure about what to do next. They had recognized one of the women. It was impossible not to know her, the naikay's wife. They had only heard rumours about the woman and now those stories were confirmed. They somehow made their way out of the water and throwing all caution to the winds, sprinted for their kulhi.

~

A Santhal man who lived two doors down from the naikay saw, one night, a strange creature in his garden. It was white, its upper limbs were disproportionately long and its eyes were large and round. It was swinging from the lowermost branch of an edel tree. At first, the man thought it was a child. But how could a child reach the branch even though it was the lowermost on the tree? And why would a child be alone in the garden at night?

The man had come out to urinate. It must have been ten at night. Ten, in those days, was as good as midnight. People ate their supper and slept early so that they could get up at daybreak. This man, too, had been in deep slumber when his bladder had awoken him. He had come out scratching his crotch, feeling his penis harden as urine filled it up, expecting the night to be silent. He would urinate in peace, hop back into the house, bolt the door and hop back into the world of dreams. He hadn't even brought a harkane lantern or a diba. Only the moon lighted his way, white, cold, forbidding.

The man had half emptied his bladder, standing under the edel tree, when he realized that the night was not silent after all. And he was not alone. He looked up, and what he saw would remain etched in his memory till his death some forty years later.

'Hey! Who are you, kid?' He asked the question with urgency, but more out of worry for the child than out of fear.

The creature stopped swinging. Then the man noticed its long arms and began to shiver. The creature jumped down from its perch and, as quick as a startled chameleon, shot into the bushes. He followed, intrigued. When he separated the leaves of the bush, a pair of large eyes with no irises stared back at him; the creatures had only two holes to breathe through; and its mouth was so small, it seemed as if the lips had been stitched tight to one another.

The curious man almost fell backwards in horror. The creature leaped like it had grown springs under the soles of its feet, jumped towards the naikay's house, and disappeared.

He recalled the events of the night to other men in the morning.

'So you saw it?' they asked him, their mouths agape.

'Why? What was it?' he asked, feeling giddy with terror.

'It was the Dhonkundra-bhoot!' they all said.

~

The effect the Dhonkundra-bhoot had on the naikay could be clearly seen in his failing health. He looked far older than many of the oldest men and women of the village. His skin was wrinkled, his stomach seemed to have been gouged out, and his back was bent. He had only one child, a son in his early teens. But the sickly boy seemed not a day older than ten. However, it wasn't as if Sima-Bonga was giving the naikay richer crops than other farmers, it hadn't magically increased the size of his holdings. He grew the same quantity of rice each year, the portion he doled out to the sharecroppers remained the same, and the bullocks had to plough the fields the same number of times each year.

Perhaps it has something to with the name, Somai-haram thought. The naikay was a Marndi, who are supposed to have the largest landholdings, the most servants, and more money than others. Marndi-kisar they are called, the rich Marndi. Not that the system follows this rule—some people with the Marndi surname are poorer than the poorest. But others take their name quite seriously. Like the naikay, for instance, who would go to any lengths to increase his wealth. But Somai-haram thought: His wife is carrying a second child. It won't be courteous to discuss witchery, the Dhonkundra-bhoot or my wife's miscarriages at this time. And anyway, such things are better not discussed. That is what has been done over the years. Santhal men drink haandi, Santhal women practise dahni-bidya, and no one speaks about it. It is as natural as the wind blowing through the trees in a sarjom grove, as water flowing in the Kadamdihi stream. Somai-haram decided to keep quiet, pray to the gods and hope for the best.

~

Older Somai-budhi conceived for the fourth time. In her eighth month, Somai-haram had a dream. In the dream, Somai-haram saw his wife sitting under the dogor tree in the backyard.

The tree is in full bloom. Flowers blossom on nearly every branch, the petals are as white as milk but the bases of the flowers are yellow, as if they have been touched by turmeric-stained fingers. Though it starts with beauty, the dream soon makes Somai-haram anxious, for he can't place the dream in his calendar, or in the usual order of things. There are flowers on the dogor tree, though the season of dogor blossoms—the rains and the late rainy season, the months of Saan and Bhador—is long over. In the dream, more than a month has passed after Sohrai, the autumn harvest festival. Winter seems to have set in and a light mist covers the entire village.

Only one image in the dream soothes Somai-haram: Older Somai-budhi basking in the meagre sun. The ground beneath her is polished smooth with cow dung and swept clean so that there is not even a stray twig in sight. There, surrounded by plenty—a kharai stacked with bales of hay left over after the threshing, a garden with a healthy crop of radish and clusters of kardi-arak—and comfortable in the silent contentment born of the assurance that she will, after all, have the privilege of becoming a mother, sits Older Somai-budhi, leisurely running the comb through her oiled tresses, soaking in the sunrays. Somai-haram looks at her from the door which opens into the backyard and happiness and apprehension churn inside him in equal measure. Older Somai-budhi is oblivious to her surroundings and to those watching her. She looks dreamily at the prickly stumps of rice plants left over after harvest in the fallows before her, and then at the faraway grove of trees surrounding the village pond.

At that moment, Somai-haram notices a shadow fall on his wife's back. It is the shadow of a woman; the afternoon sun magnifies it into an intimidating size. The shadow engulfs Older Somai-budhi completely but still she sits oblivious. Somai-haram is jolted into action. He steps out of the door and at the same time the woman comes into view. He cannot see her face; her back is turned towards him. The back seems familiar. He rushes outside. The woman—who hasn't sensed that Somai-haram is behind her—raises her hands to grab Older Somai-budhi. Somai-haram sees her hands, her fingers. Just as she is gathering herself to pounce on an unsuspecting Older Somai-budhi, Somai-haram jumps on her.

He didn't get to touch her skin; he didn't get to grab the raised, outstretched hands. Instead, Somai-haram woke up sweaty and breathless in the cold winter night. He had thrown away the kantha with which he had covered himself. The kantha on which he was sleeping was soaked with his perspiration. Close to him, his wife snored lightly, their child inside her a bulge which moved up and down with her breaths. He lay back, relieved. He tried to sleep, but couldn't. He drew the kantha over himself and kept staring at the ceiling.

The dream returned. Two days later, and then three days later. He saw it in several versions. The idyllic opening remained the same but, each time, Somai-haram's responses to the crisis changed. One night, he saw himself pouncing upon the huge woman. On another night he heard himself cry out loudly to warn his wife. On the third night he willed himself to dream longer so that he could see the face of the woman and ended up pinning her to the ground. However, the identity of the woman remained unrevealed.

The naikay's wife was as amiable as ever with Somai-haram. Occasionally, she would smile at him and ask, 'Hyan babu, ched leka? Baahu ched leka?' Though she was much younger than Somai-haram, the naikay's wife was quite friendly with him. Her position as the elder sister-in-law gave the naikay's wife authority. She was as good as an equal to all the important men in the village. She conducted herself with confidence, spoke kindly with one and all and, in awkward situations like when she had to speak with a man who was older than her but was socially her junior, she maintained decorum. The naikay's wife knew that Somai-haram was older than her, but since he was younger than her husband, she had to treat him like a younger brother-in-law. She had to call him babu. But even the word babu, when uttered by the naikay's wife for Somai-haram, was suffused with respect befitting an older man.

And while Somai-haram admired the naikay's wife for her social skills, he wondered if this affable woman was the one who had been haunting him night after night. Since he couldn't be certain, he did not tell anyone about his dream.

In the meantime, Older Somai-budhi reached the day of parturition. It was a complicated delivery. The Kunkal women clucked their tongues when they heard Older Somai-budhi's screams in their kulhi. They prayed for her. This time, the curse took the mother and spared the child. Older Somai-budhi delivered a healthy girl child but bled to death. The bleeding just wouldn't stop. Such big balls of clot—red, lumpy, smelling of metal and ordure—kept pouring out of Older Somai-budhi's body. Finally, she fought a spell of breathlessness which lasted close to an hour-and-a-half, mumbled incoherently, and then breathed her last.

In the absence of a mother, the infant was juggled from one female relative to another. Unable to decide on a proper name, they called her Putki, after a long-dead aunt of one of Somai-haram's cousins. The name was easy, and it was intended that they would use Putki first as a nickname and then as the bhitir-nyutum. They expected Somai-haram to give the child her own name once he emerged from his grief. 'Putki! Putki!' they called out to the baby. They took her in their laps and cooed, 'Putki-mai! Putki-mai!' The child took to the name so lovingly that it stuck. The girl became Putki for life.

All this while, Somai-haram deliberated over whether he should bring home another wife or not. The pressure this time was immense. Right from the moment Older Somai-budhi's corpse crackled and shrivelled to ashes in the towering flames in Somai-haram's family crematorium—quite close to where her foetuses were buried—he had been hearing whispers. 'What will happen to the child?' 'What about the baby?' 'An only daughter!' The pressure to bring home a second wife was as heavy as the pressure had been—till Older Somai-budhi carried her fourth pregnancy to full term—to adopt a child. Very tactfully, the matter was placed before him by concerned relatives. 'Putki needs a mother.' 'An engaat-tooer girl!' Finally, a few months after Putki had turned one and had her naming ceremony, Somai-haram brought her a second mother: Younger Somai-budhi.

Younger Somai-budhi was neither young nor was she unmarried. She was a widow whose husband, an acquaintance of Somai-haram's, had died more than ten years ago. Driving away a herd of wild elephants from his farm one night, he had been trampled underfoot. At the time, they had been married for just a little over a year. Issueless, Younger Somai-budhi had returned to her father's house where she, for reasons best known to her, had resisted remarriage. Instead, she had learnt from her Mahlay friends—much to her Santhal family's astonishment—the art of weaving bamboo strips into household objects such as baskets, plates and sieves.

The Mahlay tribe is separate from the Santhal, but the two share some surnames. While Santhals are a farming community, Mahlays don't own farmland and making and selling objects made from bamboo strips is their chief occupation. Mahlays allow marriage between blood relations, like between cousins, a practice which is severely looked down upon by Santhals. Some Mahlays speak Santhali, although in their very distinct Mahlay accent, which many Santhals find funny. Most Mahlays, however, speak a crude version of Bengali. As for religion, most Mahlays have given up Sarna and follow Hinduism and consider themselves Hindus. Santhals consider themselves to be straightforward in their dealings and quite honest, but think of the Mahlays as shrewd people with the gift of the gab. Younger Somai-budhi's association with the Mahlays raised many eyebrows.

Younger Somai-budhi, however, wove, gathered snails from the village pond, worked on her brothers' farms and uttered not one extra word. Silence became a way of life for her. A decade passed thus, and then a few more years. Younger Somai-budhi kept to her routine and to her silence, not raising her eyes, not listening in on conversations which did not concern her. Until someone mentioned Somai-haram and his search for a wife to look after his daughter, his beloved engaat-tooer. When she was asked if she would like to be married again to a respectable, elderly widower, she surprised everyone by nodding yes.

Somai-haram's second marriage ceremony was much simpler than his first. It was a simple tunki-dipil marriage in which he did not even have to go to Younger Somai-budhi's house. That visit was made by the custodians of the village: the majhi, the jogmajhi and the godeth who, along with the village elders, went to Younger Somai-budhi's house, paid the gonong of three rupees in cash, and returned with the bride. The remaining parts of the marriage ceremony, the sindradaan and the ritual lifting of the bridegroom and the bride, were held in Somai-haram's house in Kadamdihi. Two of Somai-haram's kinsmen—both of whom were older than Somai-haram but were still strong—lifted him on their shoulders. Two of Somai-haram's older cousins carried Younger Somai-budhi on a dowrah.

Somai-haram's second marriage was very different from his first. When he married Older Somai-budhi, it had been the ideal wedding. The gonong he had paid then was a bull calf and a heifer along with three rupees. The logic behind giving cattle is that when a man takes away a woman as his bride, he takes away a working member from the family. In giving cattle as gonong, the parents are compensated for the loss of a pair of hands on the farm. Santhals, being an agrarian community, consider cattle an asset.

Putki was kept away from the ceremony as it is considered inauspicious for children to see their parents getting married. Everyone understood the practicality of this hurried event, so as soon as the wedding ended, and the men went out to celebrate with haandi and mutton chakhna, Younger Somai-budhi was shown the kitchen by the older women of the majhi-gushti.

'Baahu,' she was told, 'you have been brought here only to keep this place in order and to raise this girl.'

Younger Somai-budhi nodded yes. She was a skilful housekeeper and manager of resources and took over the household quickly and easily. Her biggest challenge, however, was Putki, and she failed to become the mother that people expected her to be. Handling the child when she was young was easy. But as Putki grew up and found her way out of the house, she refused to accept Younger Somai-budhi's authority. 'You're not my mother,' Putki would say. 'My mother is dead. You can't tell me what I should do.'

This was the ignominy which Younger Somai-budhi faced from the day Putki learned to carry herself on her own and roamed the village listening to all and sundry about who the woman in her house was. The fact that it was her stepmother who taught her how to walk and carry herself, and who showed her around the village, did not matter to her. She was stubborn, wayward and unstoppable. Younger Somai-budhi hardly ever raised her voice, expressing herself only with her eyes, and Putki was deaf to signs and body language. Somai-haram was so immersed in religion, society, and his farm that his daughter's upbringing was hardly his concern. Younger Somai-budhi failed with Putki at every step and wondered why it was that she had chosen to marry Somai-haram.

They had said that Somai-haram's first wife had left behind a daughter, a mere infant. That infant had drawn her to become Somai-haram's second wife. She knew she couldn't have babies of her own, that was one of the conditions for her marriage—Somai-haram did not want any more children. Marrying a man with a baby was the only way she could realize her dream of raising a child.

Yet, Younger Somai-budhi was strong, and she never shed a tear at her ineptitude with Putki. She spent her time alone, never socializing more than was needed, speaking even fewer words than ever before. At home, they all slept separately. Putki took the biggest room, like the mistress of the house that she was. Somai-haram slept alone in his room, following a very strict regimen of diet, sleep, exercise and religious ritual. Younger Somai-budhi slept like a servant in the corner of a small room near the front door and the byre. That was where they stored the paddy, and she remained curled up in her corner, in the stench of dung, amidst scampering rats and mice which hopped from one baandi to the other like the Dhonkundra-bhoot.

Dular Gaatay, Reyar-Baha

Putki's best friend in Kadamdihi was Della. Della was the daughter of the naikay, his second child who was born twelve years after his son. The son was now grown up and married, but the couple was unable to have a child. He remained as weak as ever and, unable to perform any hard labour, stayed mostly at home. It was the naikay's wife, daughter-in-law and Della who attended to the family's farms, negotiated with the labourers and supervised their work.

Della was four years older than Putki. No one could tell what drew Putki to Della, a girl whose parents were infamous throughout the village for worshipping the god who brings misfortune. Perhaps it was because Somai-haram and the naikay were neighbours. It could also have been because Somai-haram was unconcerned about his daughter's upbringing. Whatever the reason, this was a pair no one from the majhi-gushti approved of.

'Chhinar!' the women of the majhi-gushti called Della. At eighteen, she had her mother's flawless ebony complexion, her height and her build, a pretty face and huge breasts, the bases of which perpetually itched because they were so large. Della put her thumbs under her breasts and scratched like there was no tomorrow. When Della's scratching threw the small anchar of her sari to one side and heaved her breasts, whoever saw her scratch would be transported to another world. Della's mother, the naikay's wife, often sang of a young woman who had bloomed like a fragrant flower and whom men drooled over. 'Kiya baha mohay a-kan; kora maylay-maylay.' It was Della, her daughter, who had become a kiya baha, and whose fragrance had spread far and wide around Chakuliya. Before she turned twenty, Della had already been with two men and Putki, following her best friend's lead, had taken as many lovers.

'Daari! Kusbi!' These were the vicious words used by the holier-than-thou women of the majhi-gushti for the promiscuous friends. 'This Della will take the naikay family down,' the women would predict. 'This is what happens when you pray to the bad gods. The naikay's son is a weakling. He has been married for so long but he can't have children. And this Della is no better than those byebsi-maiju! Only Chando-Bonga knows which man she is going to elope with.' Somewhat wistfully, the women mused, 'How did our Putki come to be involved with such a woman?'

They blamed her stepmother, Younger Somai-budhi, for failing at her task. But they had always disapproved of her poverty and her widowhood, and had always considered her entry into the majhi-gushti to be a miracle.

'What would such a woman know?' they scoffed. 'This woman from a lengta-orak! They have never had enough to eat. Had she ever seen a house so big? Or farms so huge? Their house is ekta-ghor-ekta-pinda. That's all they have. And all his life her father has worked as a mere farmhand.'

'Didn't her father and brothers give her food to eat that she had to make theka and chala like those Mahlays? And she does not speak a word. And didn't you say that she gathered snails with those Mahlay women and sold them at haats?'

'Look, she's not your mother,' they maliciously whispered to the impressionable Putki. 'Your mother is dead. You understand? Dead. This woman is a karmi-kuri your father has brought home to cook and clean for you. You must treat her like one.'

The lesson stayed, and Putki strayed. Younger Somai-budhi perhaps understood what was happening. But she herself had come to believe that she wasn't Somai-haram's wife. Somai-haram was the peak of the highest mountain in the world. She couldn't climb so high. She was indeed a servant, an ordinary karmi-kuri.

~

Della would come to Putki's house each morning and off they would go. They plucked mangoes and guavas when they were in season, swam in the Kadamdihi stream and played chok-oshta and hopscotch with the older girls who herded cattle on the banks of the stream. When they grew up, the two would stand by the main road with the other older girls and chat up the dark, muscular, sweat-soaked young men who would be returning after working on their farms or the mills in Chakuliya.

'Chhi! Chhi! These girls are a disgrace,' the women of Kadamdihi, especially those from the majhi-gushti, would say. 'The naikay's wife is a shameless woman, but what is Younger Somai-budhi doing?'

Younger Somai-budhi was bleeding. Perhaps it was the heartbreak. Or the sense of failure. A daughter of a farmhand, she had been made the wife of a member of the majhi-gushti of Kadamdihi. And what had she done in return? Nothing. The pain in her loins, the spotting she observed at times on her monochrome saris were the price Younger Somai-budhi was paying for her failure.

As if the village had not been scandalized enough by the pair's behaviour, Della went to work for a rice mill in Chakuliya as a labourer. And as if *that* were not enough, Putki tagged along. Each morning they would wake up, tie their best saris low at the waist, polish their faces with talc, oil, plait and adorn their hair with red ribbons, pack soray-daaka in tall aluminium tiffin carriers and leave for the rice mill in a gaggle of giggling girls.

Arak-phita baha ko
Chakuriya-bajar kaami-kuri-ko

They all tie their hair with red ribbons
These young women
Who work in the Chakuliya bazaar

With their jobs came money and freedom. They bought more saris and cosmetics; they made trips to various patas, gaayaans and other gatherings, where they downed glass after glass of haandi and matkom paura and met many men. Most of them lusted for the ebony-skinned, full-breasted Della, while some were attracted by the slender, fair-by-Santhal-standards Putki.

There came a point when Putki and Della stopped addressing each other by their names. Keeping in mind the four-year age gap between them, Della used to call Putki 'Putki-mai' and Putki used to call Della 'Della-dai'. However, times were changing. There was excitement and promise in the air. In Chakuliya, wherever Della and Putki went, people said that the country was free. They said that the Ingrej had left and that the sarkaar would be run by our own people. Much more exciting than national freedom was the prospect of a separate land for the hor people, for the Adivasis. At patas, at gaayaans, wherever young Santhal men and women gathered, they could hear the name of Jaipal Singh.

Jaipal Singh was a Munda from Khunti in Ranchi. He had studied at Oxford University and had captained the Indian hockey team which won gold in the 1928 Olympics held in

Amsterdam. Singh founded the Adivasi Mahasabha in 1938 which demanded a separate state called Jharkhand for the Adivasis of the Chota Nagpur region. The Adivasi Mahasabha was renamed the Jharkhand Party after Independence. Jaipal Singh was a member of the Constituent Assembly of India and he had asked for reservations to be granted to Adivasis all over India. Everyone respectfully called him Marang-Gomkay—the Big Gentleman.

Ho Santar Mahlay Munda
Abo jhoto bowak runda

Ho, Santhal, Mahlay and Munda
We all purr together, like the civet
Which we call the runda

Della and Putki heard this anthem on the roads, the song which would unite the chief Adivasi communities of the region: Ho, Santhal, Mahlay and Munda. Jharkhand, the hihiri-pipiri, the utopia which the Adivasis of the Chota Nagpur region had been striving for for so long seemed within reach, like a ripe guava hanging from the lowermost branch of a tree, brought down low by its own weight. Just stand on your toes, stretch your arm and pluck it.

With promises blooming around them and romance having taken over their lives, how could Della and Putki remain unaffected? The two maidens found an endearing term with which to address one another, a term they picked up at a gaayaan in a village near Chakuliya. Reyar-Baha—Winter Flower.

E-gaatay Reyar-Baha
E-dular Reyar-Baha

O my friend Winter Flower
O my beloved Winter Flower

That is how they addressed one another. Delicately. As if they were nymphs from heaven. Whether they were in the village, or travelling to work, or at work, or casting naughty glances at men at a pata, it was always: 'Reyar-Baha, e-gaatay Reyar-Baha.'

Della would stand outside Putki's door each morning and coo earnestly like a cuckoo in heat: 'E-dular Reyar-Baha, don't delay. We have a long way to go.'

Putki would rush out, dressed to kill, arranging her anchar with one hand and carrying her tiffin in the other, and say, 'Cho gaatay Reyar-Baha.'

The men and women of Kadamdihi could only stare.

Of the men that Della met at the patas, one was called Tira. He was from Horoghutu and was the best-looking man in his village.

Horoghutu falls midway between Chakuliya and Kadamdihi but it is some distance away from the main road. Kadamdihi and Horoghutu are not directly connected, and if one intends to travel from Chakuliya to Kadamdihi via Horoghutu, one has to make a fairly long detour. Horoghutu means the 'bank of the tortoise'. However, just as Kadamdihi had no kadam trees, Horoghutu had no horo in its ponds and streams. There were, perhaps, old men and women in that village who, after drinking haandi, could tell stories about how they would once kill tortoises and make delicious stew from their flesh, but no one had heard anyone say anything about the tortoises of Horoghutu.

Tira was handsome. Magnetic, even. He was tall, had broad shoulders, muscular arms and large eyes. His dark body had been burnished by the heat of the earth. He was a Tudu, a typical Tudu-kora-rusika, with charm enough to attract women like flies. Young women listened to him as if he were a messenger from Marang-Buru himself who had come to teach them the art of love.

'Girls, I am like the bark of the karam tree,' he would tell his admirers, who would giggle shyly and eye him from the corners of their eyes. They wanted to meet his eyes, but would become self-conscious at the very last moment. Yet when he pounded the tamak and the tumdak at festivals, the same shy women would compete with one another to fall into rows and move to Tira's intricate beats.

'They are made for each other,' the women of Kadamdihi said about his pairing with Della. 'Bengaad-jaang ar maarich-jaang.'

Tira was an orphan who had been raised by relatives in Horoghutu. He lived in their house, worked on their farms, and herded their cattle and goats. It made no sense for the bajar-kaami-kuri-ko of Kadamdihi and nearby villages to venture off the main road and make a detour through Horoghutu. But that was what they would do.

It would be quite late. The young guti-kora-ko of Horoghutu would be lounging outdoors on summer evenings, smoking bidis, laughing and chatting about women, tuning the strings of their baanaam, singing songs, relaxing after a long day of work or, after having drunk a glass or two of cool, refreshing haandi, be waiting for dinner.

The gaggle of bajar kaami-kuri-ko would enter the main kulhi of Horoghutu innocuously, as if they were visitors just passing through. They too would be tipsy, and they would be singing one of the songs which were then popular in the patas.

E-hopon-mai, hopon-mai
Silda-pata dom chalak-a se bang?

Young girl, my dear young girl
Will you go with me to the pata in Silda?

The men, lazing around on cots and tuning the strings of their baanaam, would be waiting for this song. They would spring to their feet and run, leaving everything behind. Baanaam, bidi, everything. Some of them would even untie their dhotis and fling them aside so that they wouldn't trip.

'Saab kopay, ya! Saab kopay!' they would shout to one another.

Each one would catch up with his inamorata. Tira with Della and Salkhu with Putki. Each pair would wander off to secluded corners outside the village: behind a bush, or under a shady tree, or a wide patch in a fallow—romance under moonlight. The men would squeeze the buttocks of their women and finger their nipples. The women would caress the bodies of their men, tickle their nipples, pull their erect penises out of their dhotis. The fallows outside Horoghutu would be filled with the moans and shrieks of rapture.

As the guti-kora-ko would pant themselves empty into the bajar kaami-kuri-ko, younger boys from the village—boys who were yet to come of age, or those who had attained puberty but were yet to take a woman—would spy on these men and women, they would feel the excitement racing through their own bodies, and all would wait for the day when they, too, would be old enough to have a woman.

One evening, some young boys climbed up the tree under which Tira and Della usually made love. Tira was their hero; they'd spied upon him many times with other women. And each time had been more exciting than the last.

Della seemed to be more excited of the two, and it seemed as if she would eat up Tira whole. Where on Tira's body didn't she run her lips and tongue? Tira raised his arms and Della licked his armpits too. She then untied his dhoti and took his penis in her mouth. Aroused, Tira stripped the frenzied Della.

'Adi babat meya-se?' he asked, cupping her breasts in his hands.

'Y...yes... Yes.' Della could hardly speak from excitement.

'I'll cure your itch, then,' Tira said and licked her breasts, slurping on her nipples, nibbling on them.

'Alo, bidhwa!' Della protested between harsh sighs and held on to Tira.

'Should I stop? Huh!' Tira slapped her cheeks. Once, twice, left cheek, right cheek. Yet Della embraced him even tighter.

He stopped playing with her breasts and reached down. Tira pinched her pubic hair and pulled. He then fingered her vagina and Della began screaming, her voice a mix of pain and pleasure.

'Alo-se! Alo-se! Bidhwa-rapad!' she groaned.

'Haape, maiju! Hudung ligyin,' Tira panted as he plunged his fingers inside her.

'Bidhwa-rapad! Aaa... Bidhwa-rapad!' Della shouted and tried to drag Tira upon her.

The young boys on the tree couldn't understand how Della could enjoy what Tira was doing and yet abuse him so unmercifully.

'Thir kot me, maiju! Der lagid-em gujut kana? Nongka lang der meya, phet-phetaw hocho meyalang!' Tira scolded Della, turned her on her stomach, and slapped her buttocks.

And even though Della abused Tira, she was like clay in his hands. He pulled her up on all fours, kneaded her fleshy buttocks and ran his finger up and down between the buttocks.

'Imainj me se!' Della turned around and took Tira's penis in her hand.

'Haape, maiju!' Tira said, pulling away from her hands, and entered her from behind even as he pinned her down with his bulk.

'Ayu...! Goij kidin-ay, na! Bidhwa-rapad! Jalchhindar!' Della shouted so loudly in pain, it was a miracle the boys did not fall out from the tree.

Taking advantage of a brief moment when Tira drew himself

out, Della succeeded in turning around. She took Tira's engorged penis in her hand.

'Nye! Chopoj me! Adi chopoj sana yek meya!' Tira stood up and gave Della his organ; he loomed large, a dark giant in the moonlight. Della took him in her mouth and began sucking.

Tira sighed hard. 'Maiju, chaba kidin-am!' he muttered.

The spying boys could feel their hearts leap about; their mouths dried up and filled with a strange chemical taste. They tightly held on to branches lest they fell off. Tira and Della rolled over each other and grabbed at whatever they could lay their hands on. They groaned and abused each other like the boys had never heard before. Some of them ejaculated up there on the tree even as they held on to the branches for dear life. It was no wonder that Tira was their hero. He was what they wanted to become when they grew older.

The rolling stopped. Della raised both her legs upwards, folded her knees and, grabbing Tira's taut buttocks with her hands, controlled his rhythm.

'Engamem…! Engamem…! Engamem…!' Tira muttered as he ejaculated into Della.

'Tira-rapad! Tudu-rapad! Tira-chotod! Tira-bidhwa…!' Della muttered as she climaxed.

Elsewhere in the fallows just outside Horoghutu, other couples would be engaged in similar encounters. Once they finished, the women would gather around and walk away in a group, happy and singing louder than before.

~

It was certain that Della would marry Tira. But the one question on everybody's minds was who would Putki marry? Would she wantonly disregard her father's position and pick any man off the haat-pata to elope with? Or would she settle down with a man chosen for her by her father? Each morning, the people of Kadamdihi woke up with the questions: Which man will Putki marry? And if she won't marry soon, how many men will she be with before settling down?

But it soon became clear that Putki had chosen a man for herself. Salkhu was related to another landed family of Horoghutu. He, too, looked after the farm and the animals. As far as looks went, he wasn't a patch on Tira. But they were the best of friends and were constantly together, just as Della and Putki were. So when Della and Tira chose each other, Putki, too, chose the best friend of her best friend's lover.

Even as all these exciting developments were happening in the friends' lives, Della's mother—the naikay's wife—was getting worried about the step her daughter was going to take. She needed a successor, someone to carry her witchery forward. According to her, it should only be a matter of time before Della followed in her footsteps and roamed naked on the banks of the Kadamdihi stream, looking for maanmi-gurij to eat. Although all she had to do was to whisper the adhai-koli montro into Della's ears, or trace the montro on her open, unsuspecting palm, she could not manage to. And Della seemed to be slipping out of her hands.

Those residents of Kadamdihi who had nothing to do with the occult said to one another. 'Whatever she does, one can only hope she doesn't pass on her knowledge to Della. She is such a nice girl.'

For Della might drink hooch and haandi like a man, she might be called a whore, but on the inside, she was one of the best women the village had ever seen. Della spoke her mind, she never lied about her whereabouts or about anything else, believed in the good gods, and was always ready to help those in need. At times, it was Della's benign smile which took away the worries of many people. Like that old Kamar man who had lost his heifer.

~

It was a rainy afternoon after a particularly humid night and day in the month of Saan. The mood in the village was as sullen as the weather, especially in the Kamar-kulhi where tempers were usually as hot as the iron that glowed in the forges and flew about as easily as flecks of ash. The Kamar women had tongues which were sharper than the scythes their men created.

This old Kamar man—weakened by age in both arm and eye—had been given charge of the animals of the family. While his sons managed the smithy and their wives ran the household, this old man went out to graze the cattle and goats. That morning he had taken the animals out to graze when it began to rain. The downpour made them hurry home and in the melee he somehow managed to lose a heifer. All hell broke loose when he reported the incident. While the sons chose to remain quiet, their wives did not.

'Bedhua-mora! Gouge your eyes out if you can't see a whole cow! Where have you lost her? Go! Go and bring her back. Or else you can forget that you have a house to eat and live in.'

Dejected, the old man went out into the pouring rain, a tattered umbrella in his hand. His little grandchildren ran behind him, pulled at his drenched dhoti, pinched his buttocks and called him names.

The old man walked the entire length of the Kamar-kulhi though he realized how futile it was. He hadn't taken the animals into the village so there was no question of the heifer being there. Yet he tried to convince himself that the heifer must have strayed into someone's house. So he went from house to house and people called out to him.

Hansda Sowvendra Shekhar

'What happened, budha? Why are you out in this rain?'

'I have lost my heifer,' the old man replied meekly. 'Have you seen her?'

'Your heifer?' one Kamar man asked. 'You lost her in the morning and you're looking for her now, in this rain? The Saotals must have roasted and eaten her up. Go! Go back home. You'll die of cold.'

'Your heifer?' another Kamar man said. 'You are out looking for her in this rain? You'll die of cold, you foolish old man. Go home. Go! Go! Look for your heifer tomorrow. Or wait till the rain stops, she'll come back home on her own. Animals remember their tracks. Go! Go back home.'

'If only I could,' the old man muttered and walked towards the Kadamdihi stream, for that was where he had grazed his cattle. On the way, amidst the patter of raindrops, he heard approaching laughter—reckless, uninhibited, carefree. Then he saw them, the fairies of the village, the notorious Della and Putki, draped in drenched kachas too small to cover their bodies, huddled under a single umbrella, unconcerned about the foul weather, laughing and chatting merrily.

'Ki khobor, daadu?' Della cheerfully greeted the old man. 'Are you going for a swim, too? It's wonderful, daadu. If you're going that way, you must take a dip.'

'Bless you, children,' the old man said meekly. 'But I'm in no mood for a swim.'

'Then what business do you have in this weather?' Della asked in mock anger, standing with her arms akimbo. 'What could be more wonderful than taking a dip in our Kadamdihi stream?'

'I've lost my heifer,' he said, almost in tears.

'Oh! That's the matter?' Della said. 'Then you must surely go down to the stream. We saw a heifer there standing under the omori shrubs. She must be yours. Go, take a look. And don't forget to swim.'

The old man's face shone with pleasure. He blessed Della and Putki again and rushed off. And there she was! The heifer. His heifer. He blessed Della some more, and on his way home, dragging the heifer behind him, he blessed her again. And again. Till he reached home. In all his life, no one had talked to him so tenderly. Not his wife, who had been dead for more than ten years; not his sons; not their wives, certainly; not his grandchildren; not even his long-dead, now-forgotten mother.

Others had other impressions of Della. Of her grace, of her honeyed voice and kind words, of her bright, beatific smile. No one wanted her to lead a life like her mother's, of sin and secret knowledge. Della did not want it either. So many times had the Dhonkundra-bhoot made its presence felt to her, and every visit had ended in disaster. But for the bhoot, not the fearless Della.

~

She had walked out into their garden one night to relieve herself. It was a beautiful konami night, much like the one in which their neighbour had spotted the bhoot in his garden. Della opened the door and there it was, sitting on its haunches, staring at her.

'Durr!' Della, half-awake and unafraid, shooed the bhoot away. It scampered off. She walked to a corner of the garden where the jasmine vines touched the ground. There, behind the screen of the vines, she prepared to squat. She had lifted the hem of her sari and petticoat when the Dhonkundra-bhoot came scampering up, demanding her attention. It leaped high and perched on a branch above Della's head. It curled its legs around the branch and hung upside down, staring at Della, its eyes like two large mirrors above her head.

Anyone else would have fled. But Della being Della, stood up straight, looked up at the bhoot and said sternly, 'If you don't let me piss on the ground, I'll piss in your mouth.'

The bhoot jumped back to the ground. Maybe it understood what she said, maybe it was offended. Della did not care. 'Durr!' she shooed it away again, but it shuffled close to Della who was, by now, losing her patience. She walked close to the bhoot so that she could almost touch it, raised the hem of her sari and tucked it around her waist. The bhoot stared at her legs.

'How shameless you are! My father has tamed you; I am your sister. And what are you doing?' Saying this, she kicked the Dhonkundra-bhoot on its forehead, right between its eyes.

The bhoot yelled shrilly as it rolled away like a football. Aaaaaaaa… it screamed. Humans, of course, couldn't hear it scream. But birds and animals can catch vibrations. As soon as the Dhonkundra-bhoot screamed, all the birds roosting in the trees in the naikay's garden flew from their nests and made such a racket, it seemed as if the world was about to end. 'E-ba! E-ba!' the bhoot cried, leaped high, and jumped back inside the naikay's house. Della returned to her corner and squatted in peace.

Relieved, she had entered the house when her father came hobbling up and stopped her. 'Why did you do that?'

'Why don't you ask him why he was staring at me?'

'The god is not to be questioned,' the naikay roared with whatever strength he could muster.

'And I am not to be stared at.' Saying this, Della waved her father aside and walked across the courtyard to her room.

'I'll lock you up inside your room,' the naikay shouted. 'Then I'll see what you do.'

She stopped, turned around, walked back to her father, looked him in the eyes and said, 'There are many things even I can do to you but I don't, because you are my father. Don't forget.'

~

Two months later, she packed her clothes and shifted to Horoghutu where Tira married her. Her parents did not attend the wedding, though the majhi and the elders of Horoghutu, and two of Tira's uncles, came to Kadamdihi and—in the presence of the majhi and the elders of Kadamdihi—paid the gonong. Tira's family was very happy with their new daughter-in-law. And everyone in Kadamdihi was happy with the match, except the naikay's family. The majhi had a tough time convincing the naikay of Tira's goodness and two meetings had to be called between the moray-ko of the two villages. Ultimately, the naikay came around and blessed the couple, though half-heartedly.

Even though Putki had been excited about Della's marriage, she lost her good cheer soon after Della left. Putki's sadness gripped Younger Somai-budhi. She bled more than ever before and there was a marked hardness in her lower abdomen, of the size of a large potato, which seemed to be extending upwards. She also started stinking of fish slime. Those in Somai-haram's house—Somai-haram himself, Putki and the servants—could stand the stink as they became used to Younger Somai-budhi's condition. But they became only used to it; no one knew what to do for her.

'Reyar-Baha,' Della said to Putki on her next visit to Kadamdihi, 'I am happy with my Tira. What will you do when I am gone?'

'Gone?' Putki asked, jolted. 'You are already gone. Where else are you planning to go?'

Della smiled. 'We are going very far,' she said, and sighed. 'Very, very far.'

'Reyar-Baha…' Putki grabbed Della's hand. 'Reyar-Baha, you…'

'Yes, Reyar-Baha.' Della sighed again. 'We'll be leaving soon. My Tira has found a job in Namal-disom. We'll be given a patch of land to farm. We'll build a house there.'

Putki stared incredulously at Della. 'Namal-disom? And what will I do then? What about me? Take me… Take me, too.'

Della held Putki's hands tightly and shook them hard. 'No, Reyar-Baha. How can we take you? You have to stay here.'

'Without you?'

'There is someone for you.'

'Who?'

'Salkhu.'

'Salkhu?'

'Yes. He likes you. Marry him. Maybe he'll bring you to me one day.'

'Salkhu?'

'Yes. Salkhu.'

~

With Della and Tira gone, Putki sank into further melancholy and Younger Somai-budhi bled even more, so much that she couldn't rise from her cot. The large potato in her abdomen grew into a grapefruit and stopped just below her ribs. It hurt her and she was sure it would burst soon.

Then, on the day Putki left, the grapefruit cracked. Everyone said it was because of Putki's leaving.

Putki had never liked Salkhu. They had had fun together but there was not a hint of love in what Putki felt for Salkhu. On every night of the one week that Putki stayed in Horoghutu with Salkhu, both of them would drink copious baatis of haandi and have drunken, violent fights. Salkhu would express his love for Putki while she would scold him at the top of her voice, refusing all his advances. Salkhu's family could only gape in astonishment.

Salkhu would slur, 'I can die for you.'

Putki would shrug him off. 'Durr! Chatyal!'

Salkhu would lose his patience and scream, 'I have kept you in my house!'

'So, do you think you own me?' Putki would reply.

Salkhu would pull Putki's hair and force himself upon her, mercilessly slapping her face and tearing off her clothes.

Putki would pummel him with her fists and grab his hair.

Ocassionally, Salkhu would cry, 'Putki... Putki... Dulariya, you are my life...'

And Putki would bawl.

The first time this happened, one of Salkhu's aunts called out to his younger cousins to check on the quarreling pair. 'Du-se, na! Nyel kin pe! It looks like they have killed each other.'

The younger cousins found Salkhu and Putki nearly naked and engaged in a tussle; weeping, screaming, shaking each other. Salkhu's dhoti was covering only one of his legs and the other was exposed from the waist downwards. Putki's blouse had been torn off and her breasts heaved violently with her struggles. Yet when the terrified cousins raised the diba and asked: 'Salkhu-dada?' Salkhu replied calmly: 'What is it? Please, go.' Putki, drunk and disoriented, laughed. 'Go away! This is nothing! Your dada was just showing me how much he loves me.'

The terrified—and scandalized—cousins scampered away.

After that, Salkhu's family left them mostly alone. At times, they were like the best of lovers, bathing together, washing each other's clothes, as playful as young children. At others, they were as vicious as a cat and a dog thrown together. If their quarrels became too loud and violent, someone wandered over to check. Otherwise they just let them fight, fuck or sleep, as they pleased.

When a party of elders from Kadamdihi visited Horoghutu to either bring Putki back or to get her respectfully married to Salkhu, Salkhu told the men that he loved Putki and that he was ready to marry her. But Putki—a bored traveller who has seen too much in too little time—told the elders that she would like to return to Kadamdihi. And on the day of her return, the grapefruit inside Younger Somai-budhi burst, killing her. She was perhaps waiting for Putki's return, waiting to see her ward safely home. It may have been that Younger Somai-budhi's disease had had an effect on the wandering Putki, and drew her home instead of letting her end up in a marriage with a man she did not like. Whatever it was, Putki's return seemed to absolve Younger Somai-budhi of all guilt. It was as if she could tell the gods that she might have been an incapable mother but not a bad one.

The Groom with One Short Leg

Occasional news about Della and Tira reached Kadamdihi from Namal-disom in the district of Bardhaman, deep in the fertile plains of Bengal. They lived in a Santhal village set up by a rich zamindar. The zamindars of Bengal employed many workers and most of them were Santhals and other Adivasis—Munda and Oraon—from Chota Nagpur. The Santhals came from Dhar-disom and Dampara-disom in Bihar; from Barha-disom, Silda-disom and Toong-disom in Bengal; even from the faraway Aatkusi-disom and Babonhati-disom in Orissa. The zamindars appointed them sharecroppers on their lands and gave them small farms. They tilled these lands on behalf of these zamindars. Della and Tira were happy with their new life.

Back home in Kadamdihi, everyone breathed a deep sigh of relief. 'Chando-Bonga is great,' they said. 'With that Della gone, some sense should now dawn on Putki. It is time Somai-haram found Putki a proper husband.'

A proper husband for Putki: that was the only thought in Somai-haram's mind. He was quite old and frail by now, shaken by the death of his dutiful, neglected wife and almost disconnected with the affairs of the village. He knew he couldn't let his daughter stray anymore and should, at all costs, take up the matter of her marriage. There was also the question of inheritance. Who would he leave his farms to? The bigger question, however, was: Would it be easy to find Putki a man from family with a status equal to theirs after all the adventures she had had?

Any man would do, he decided: a bachelor, a widower, or a divorcee. He had just three conditions: the man shouldn't be a Hansda, he shouldn't have a living wife, and Putki could not leave Kadamdihi—Somai-haram did not trust his daughter. He'd keep her husband home, in Kadamdihi, as a ghardi-jawai. However, no self-respecting man would want to become a ghardi-jawai, even if he was marrying the only daughter of a man from the majhi-gushti of Kadamdihi.

After much deliberation, Somai-haram sent out feelers all over the region. A daughter of the majhi-gushti of Kadamdihi village—a Hansda girl—seeks a husband, someone who's willing to live with her in her house. Family no bar. Interested parties may contact the girl's father in person.

It was Khorda Baskey's cartload of memories which made him accept Somai-haram's terms.

Khorda was from Lowadihi. Lowadihi—named after lowa, the fig tree—is a village some five to seven kilometres to the east of Kadamdihi, in the direction of Salbuni.

Just outside Lowadihi is the putur-dungri, a bald hillock with no vegetation and only a single taalay tree at its peak. A ravishingly beautiful jugni spirit, said to cause disease, lived under the taalay tree. Young cowherd boys would often see the jugni roam naked on top of the putur-dungri, her long, unkempt hair sweeping the ground; they would see her tend to her stock of onions, garlic and ginger which she dried on sarjom leaves under a strong sun. Fascinated by her beauty, the cowherd boys approached the jugni one day and had gotten quite near when an elderly cowherd, bent with age, stopped them. 'Hey!' he shouted. 'Why are you bothering that poor lady? Go away! Go back to your cows and goats.'

'But, grandfather,' one of the boys asked, 'why is she naked? Who is she?'

'No one, no one.' The man waved his long, thick staff. 'Go away before I give each of you a thrashing.'

The children ran away. The old man turned around to make his way down the putur-dungri when the jugni called out to him in a very gentle voice. 'Sir, would you be kind enough to tell me which way I should go today?'

He pointed towards Salbuni village on the other side of the hillock. 'That way. Go that way.'

The jugni nodded in gratitude, picked up a handful of garlic and threw it in the direction of Salbuni. The next morning, the people of Lowadihi heard that five men in Salbuni had, all of a sudden, been struck down by diarrhoea and vomiting. Severely dehydrated, three of them died. Even though the jugni wasn't openly discussed, the people of Lowadihi found out about the cowherds' encounter with the spirit and about her stock of dry spices. When asked, the old man confirmed the encounter with the jugni but did not say that he had sent her to Salbuni.

Khorda Baskey did not have a better name. He took pride in the name he had been given because of his physical shortcoming. Khorda's right leg was shorter than his left. Apart from that, he had a near-perfect body. Though short, he had stout arms and a broad chest, broad shoulders, and the strength of a bull. Till he learnt to walk, he had been called hopon-babu, the small boy, for he was the youngest of three brothers. But when his limp became prominent as he grew up, everyone began to call him Khorda, or lame, or Khorda-babu, and the name stayed. Gradually, the name Khorda Baskey found a place in the sarkaari papers: the family's ration card and the land deeds.

Khorda was an attractive man. Whenever he visited village fairs with friends, where men and women would dance with their hands around each other's waists, women couldn't take their eyes off him. Some of them would pull at him, and invite him to dance. Conscious of his deformity, Khorda would refuse each time. All his friends, however, would jump right in, holding on to the women of their choice, matching their steps to the beats of the tamak and the tumdak, and moving to the lilting strains of the tiriyo and the baanaam. Many of them would take off with the women they fancied, but Khorda would always stay behind, always alone. He could not get over his inhibitions even after drinking many glasses of haandi and paura. For this, his friends would jeer him for being shyer than the very women they wooed. 'Cho-say, ya! Cho, cho! Adim lajak kaan do! Kuri khon hno baysee.'

Yet he exercised restraint. Until that day at the Dasai-pata which is held to mark the autumn Dashami festival. At the Dasai-pata that year, Khorda saw the most beautiful woman ever. She was standing in the row just behind the dancers. She was with her friends, though—like Khorda himself—she seemed aloof, alone in the din.

Khorda couldn't take his eyes off her even though he could only catch fleeting glimpses through the tall, peacock-feather headdresses of the male dancers. The dance happening at the time described the warriors Dibi and Durga who were rushing out of their houses to rescue their abducted lovers, Ainom and Kajol.

Haaye-re haaye-re haaye-re
Dibi ar Durga du-kin odok-ena re
Dibi ar Durga du-kin bahir-ena re
Chete do-kin odok-ena re?
Chete do-kin bahir-ena re?
Haaye-re haaye-re haaye-re
Haaye-re haaye-re haaye-re

Dibi and Durga have left their houses
Dibi and Durga have come out of their houses
Why have they left their houses?
Why have they come out of their houses?
Haaye-re haaye-re haaye-re

Some men got hold of Khorda and urged him to join the dance. He stood up, much to everyone's surprise, and his friends cheered. He acknowledged the attention and looked to where the woman was standing. But she had left. He rapidly limped out of the circle, steadying himself after every four steps, but he could not catch even a glimpse of her.

The next day, he sat near a pond outside Lowadihi, his legs in the water. Though still tipsy from the night before, he had risen early. He looked at his sad face in the pellucid water. He saw slender dandka fish shimmying in shoals, and frogs jumping from one rock to another. Even the pebbles at the bottom of the pond seemed happier than he was. None of his friends knew the woman, though they were delighted to know that he had finally found someone. They drank to his happiness, but was he really happy? He should have gone ahead and asked her her name, which village she came from, and who her father was. But he was so shy. His friends were probably right; he was shyer than a woman. The cool autumn breeze ruffled the white inflorescences of the tall kaasi quills. The kaasi was so dense, a tiger could be hiding among them and no one would know. Tigers weren't on Khorda's mind now, nor was the jugni.

'Khorda-babu,' a woman called out.

Khorda sat up, alert. Who was it? Was it the jugni? Or one of the Saat-Bohoni, the Seven Sisters who live in the depths of stagnant ponds. The Saat-Bohoni are the goddesses of ponds and lakes. It is said that their feet are turned backwards and they keep an eye out for all the young men who come to bathe. If they happen to find one attractive, they drag him to the depths of the pond. They sit the young man on a gaando of coiled serpents and feed him taaben made of dried gooseberry leaves. Then they make him their consort and seduce him so that he is forced to make love to all seven of them one after the other. The day after, the man's soulless body emerges from the depths of the pond and floats on its surface.

Khorda pulled his legs out of the water. No, he did not want to become a husband to the Seven Sisters. He did not want to be a god in the depths of a pond. He was happy on earth, on solid ground.

'Khorda-babu,' the voice called again. It had come closer. He turned around.

There she was. The beauty from the Dasai-pata.

'Khorda-babu,' she said shyly, 'I came looking for you all the way from Salbuni. My name is Dangi.'

Dangi—also one of the goddesses of the Sarna pantheon—said that she had been visiting relatives in Lowadihi, which is why no one knew her. He had been thinking about her, and she had come looking for him. He couldn't possibly send her back.

Theirs was a pair the people of Lowadihi talk about even today. It was far finer than Khorda's pair with Putki. Dangi and Khorda were made for each other. When they walked together— Khorda hobbling, Dangi respectfully controlling her stride to match steps with her man—everyone agreed that was how a man and his wife should be. And everyone still remembers how inconsolable Khorda had been when Dangi, within a year of the wedding, succumbed to an illness which left her body as yellow as turmeric.

When Khorda accepted to marry Putki, many turned up their noses. Does a butterfly like Putki deserve a sensible man like Khorda? they asked. They marvelled at Khorda's decision, too, and wondered if he had agreed to become a ghardi-jawai to escape Lowadihi and the memories of Dangi.

What surprised people even more was that Putki agreed to such a marriage. Everybody had expected the mercurial and rebellious woman to throw a fit, to perhaps run away from home once again at the prospect of marrying a widower with one short leg. But it soon became clear to all that Della had taken Putki's rebellious self away with her. It wasn't clear if Putki had become sensible or not, but it was certain that she wasn't the Putki who would talk or fight back. Some suspected it was Putki's own sense of guilt at the death of Younger Somai-budhi, a mother whose worth she never realized. Just as her stepmother had walked through life, Putki strolled into this marriage in silence.

~

An affable man, Khorda quickly made friends in Kadamdihi. It was soon widely acknowledged that despite being a widower, Khorda Baskey was the best husband Putki could have found. He was social, he knew the entire Karam-Binti—the story of the brothers Karmu and Dharmu told on the night of Karam-Bonga, in which everyone stays up all night—and the protocol to be followed at the jaher, and was ever ready to help everyone. The younger men and women in Kadamdihi fondly called him Khorda-teyang, teyang being the husband of one's elder sister.

Khorda was not only social, he was also quite aware of what was happening in the world around him. He motivated the people of Lowadihi and Kadamdihi to vote in the elections of 1952. He told them about Jaipal Singh and the Jharkhand Party. He told them about the massacre of Ho and Santhal demonstrators in Kharsawan in 1948, in which more than a thousand Adivasis were killed.

'They were our brothers,' he told friends and acquaintances in Kadamdihi. 'They were hor like us. Some were Santar like us, others were Larka. They had gathered to demand what is good for us, our rights. But police came and shot them all dead. Was that right? What was their fault? We are living in a free country now. Don't we have the right to demand what is good for us?'

He told everyone that the creation of Jharkhand was in the interest of the Adivasis. It was because of her husband that Putki—carrying young Sido in her arms—voted in the first general elections of the country and became part of history. At that time, Ghatshila, Chakuliya and Baharagora used to be part of one assembly constituency: Ghatshila-Baharagora. Because of its sheer size, both in terms of area and population, the Ghatshila-Baharagora constituency was made a double-member assembly constituency; that is, two members were chosen from there. The seat for one member was unreserved while the other seat was reserved for an Adivasi—officially called Scheduled Tribe, or ST—candidate. The Jharkhand Party contested for both seats, and such was the craving for a separate Jharkhand state, the entire constituency voted unanimously for the Jharkhand Party, stamping their choice on the party's unforgettable symbol: a proud rooster. The Jharkhand Party won both seats. Mukunda Ram Tanty was the winner of the unreserved seat while Ghaniram Santhal won the seat reserved for the ST candidate. Both made history by becoming members of the first-ever Bihar Vidhan Sabha of independent India. And not only in Ghatshila-Baharagora, the Jharkhand Party created history by also becoming the chief opposition party in the first Bihar Vidhan Sabha. Such were the times, such was the passion of the people, the desire of the Adivasis to have their own homeland.

After the elections, though, a number of issues took precedence and the question of Jharkhand was shifted to the back burner. In 1956, India was reorganized along linguistic lines. Everyone was bothered about who spoke Bihari, who spoke Bengali and who spoke Oriya. Bidhan Chandra Roy took Manbhum, the forest-rich, limestone- and iron-rich, Bengali-speaking Puruliya, away from Bihar and attached it to West Bengal. He also had his eyes on Jamshedpur, Chaibasa and Ghatshila. However, shrewd and speedy thinking by Shri Krishna Sinha kept the mineral- and forest-rich, industrialized Singhbhum from going to West Bengal. When such big barters were taking place, why would anyone bother to see who or how many spoke Santhali, Mundari, Ho or Kurukh?

Nothing changed for those parts of Bihar, West Bengal, Orissa and Madhya Pradesh which the leaders of the Jharkhand movement were trying to turn into their utopia, the land of their dreams. Similarly, nothing changed in Kadamdihi. Not even the hope that Jharkhand would one day be created and that all the Adivasis of Chota Nagpur would make their own laws and be their own rulers. That hope remained unfulfilled.

Sido was growing up, and six years after Sido, Putki had one more son: Doso. Around the time the Jaipal Singh-led faction of the Jharkhand Party merged controversially with the Indian National Congress at the behest of Jawaharlal Nehru, Somai-haram died peacefully. Young Sido poured water into his mouth from a sarjom-leaf bowl while little Doso stared curiously at the mournful looks on everyone's faces.

The New Bride Learns New Things

The prediction that Rupi's mother once made in a bullock cart many years ago—that they would get her married to a man from the majhi-gushti of Kadamdihi—finally came true when Khorda chose Rupi for Sido. Technically, Sido did not belong to the majhi-gushti because, after her marriage with Khorda Baskey, Putki had become a bride of Lowadihi. But as Khorda lived in Kadamdihi, a ghardi-jawai in his father-in-law's house, he had become one of the much respected sons-in-law of the majhi-gushti of Kadamdihi.

Sido's wedding was one of the finest Kadamdihi had ever seen. Nearly all the Santhal men went along with his bariyat to Tereldihi, on foot and in bullock carts, the distance between the two places notwithstanding. The camaraderie between the two brothers—Sido and Doso—on the day of the wedding was splendid. As his brother's lumti-kora, Doso was teased quite unmercifully by the young women of Tereldihi. But Doso was the true inheritor of his mother's traits. He pulled some of them close and pretended to put sindoor in the partings of their hair even as the women squealed with laughter.

The wedding banquet in Tereldihi was small but suffused with pride. The banquet in Kadamdihi, in Putki's house, was large and sumptuous. Seventeen pots of haandi were brewed. Eight large goats were slaughtered. Gira, the traditional Santhali wedding invitation, had been sent to guests from ten villages, and everyone attended.

Rupi lost count of the number of women who came to see her. She would have to learn fast, remember each one's face, name and how each was related to her. But she kept forgetting. 'She's an aunt,' Putki prompted. 'Lower your head, bow into her palms.' 'She's a younger cousin,' Putki prompted again. 'Cup your palms so that she can bow into them, and don't forget to bless her so that she grows up as tall as a mountain and finds a good husband.'

Soon, Rupi began to blindly follow Putki's instructions, her mind numbed by all the information.

However, of all the women who passed in front of her in an endless procession, there was one she would never forget. From the next morning onwards, she would see that woman every day, and her countenance was recorded in that space in Rupi's mind where all her happy thoughts had so far lain.

The woman she saw was old, much older than Putki. She stooped slightly at the waist and Rupi felt that had she stood up straight, the woman would surely be taller than many women and men. Her gait was swift for her age and her build suggested that she must once have been hefty. The woman could look right through her, Rupi felt. And even more strangely, her large eyeballs would not stop rolling for a single second. It was as if she wanted to keep an eye on every object in that room at all times. And when she raised her hands to bless Rupi, she saw that the fingers were mere bones, with a wrinkly sheet of skin drawn over them. 'What a pretty daughter-in-law you've got, Putki-mai,' the woman said in a raspy voice which seemed to come from the depths of a well. 'So fair, just like the dogor flower. I think I can see her sitting under the dogor tree already.'

'What are you saying, marak-ayo?' Putki asked, suddenly

alarmed. There was a smile on her face, but her voice betrayed her: the woman's words were ominous and alarming.

'Oh, nothing,' the woman said, shaking her head, as if the comment had been made in passing and could be overlooked. 'I was just saying that Sido's bride is as pretty as the dogor flower.'

'Of course she is, marak-ayo.' Putki smiled broadly. 'Baahu,' she said to Rupi, 'this is the naikay's widow. She will be like a grandmother to you. Her daughter used to be a very good friend of mine. Come, bow before her.'

As Rupi bowed, her fear subsided.

'May you live well and have many sons,' the naikay's wife said in her trapped, raspy voice.

The naikay's widow had come with her daughter-in-law; a short, dusky woman whose hair was tied up in a tight bun, the size of a gooseberry, at her occiput. She looked of the same age as Putki, maybe older, and had the same rolling eyes as her mother-in-law. Rupi wondered why their eyes rolled thus. She would soon find out.

~

Rupi took charge of the house within a fortnight of her marriage, and shouldered almost all the duties of cooking, cleaning and tending to the animals. She had Putki to help her, as well as Doso and Sonamuni, an old widowed cousin of Khorda's from Lowadihi. Sonamuni had agreed to chaperone Rupi till she got to know Kadamdihi better.

'Don't walk through the village alone, baahu,' was Sonamuni's first advice to Rupi. 'And don't eat or drink anything the naikay's widow or daughter-in-law offers you.'

Rupi did not ask any questions. Perhaps she understood, perhaps she was too shy.

Each morning she got up, dusted and made her bed, picked

up the broom and swept both the inner and the back yards. However, it was either Putki or Sonamuni who cleaned the front of the house which opened into the kulhi because they did not want to let Rupi out of the house except under their supervision. Sido had left for Nitra just three days after the wedding. He did not have more leave of absence from work.

Sido's colleague from school in Nitra, Bairam Tudu, had also attended his wedding. Sido had effusively, drunkenly praised his Bairam-da when introducing Rupi to Bairam at the wedding banquet. He had slurred, 'And this is Bairam-da. He is like my elder brother. His wife is like a mother to me. She's the one who feeds me in Nitra.'

Rupi could only drag her toenails on the ground in shame. When she had raised her eyes for a fraction of a second, she had seen that Bairam-master—as everyone called him—too had an embarrassed look on his face. It was Doso's timely intervention which had saved the moment.

Bairam had stayed over after the banquet and left early the next morning. Rupi later gathered from the gossipy Sonamuni that Bairam was from Horoghutu village. He, too, had attended the teachers' training school in Chakuliya and was a few years senior to Sido. Bairam would visit his family in Horoghutu before leaving for Nitra.

'This Horoghutu too has a story,' Sonamuni told Rupi, clucking her tongue mischievously. 'You'll know, you'll know, it'll take some time, but you will,' she said mysteriously, relishing the puzzled look on Rupi's face. Rupi, the innocent new bride that she was, couldn't understand a word of what Sonamuni said about Horoghutu and its story. She wondered if Kadamdihi was really as mysterious a village as the grove of trees outside the village made it seem. She wondered if she would have to change herself to fit in there.

From Putki, Rupi learnt that in Nitra, both Sido and Bairam-master lived in the majhi's house. The majhi had a huge house and he had given a part of it to the two teachers. One reason was that they were both Santhal. Also, Sido and Bairam helped the children of the majhi's family with their lessons. Once Sido had readied the rooms given to him, he would take Rupi along. Till then, he'd visit every Saturday, catching the afternoon passenger train to Chakuliya from the Rakha Mines Railway Station after school ended. He would then return to Nitra on Monday by the early morning local train, getting down at the Rakha Mines Railway Station and travelling to Nitra by bus in time for a quick breakfast before school. Gurubari, Bairam-master's wife, cooked all three meals of the day for both men. Once Rupi knew Sido's routine in Nitra, she started getting up early on Monday mornings to pack a meal for Sido. She would cook extra rice the night before he was to leave and reserve some of it. In the morning, she would roast and mash a brinjal, or heat up some arak from the night before, and pack it all in an aluminium tiffin box and hand it over to Sido.

The first time she did this, Sido had been surprised. 'What is this?' he'd asked.

'Food,' Rupi had answered plainly.

'Why?'

'So that you don't have to ask anyone else for it.'

Sido had left, and returned the next weekend with more questions for Rupi.

'Why do you have to do it?' he had asked her as they prepared for bed.

'It is my work.'

'Your work?' He had drawn her close. 'And what else is your work?'

Rupi had shyly let go of his hand and curled up in her corner of the bed. Sido had grabbed her from the back, slid his hand under her anchar and caressed her abdomen. Rupi, tickled and afraid, doubled up. Her buttocks, which touched Sido's crotch, had aroused him. He had lifted up her sari and had felt her legs, her thighs, and above. Rupi had been scared stiff. She had breathed heavily and when Sido kissed her full on her mouth, his hairy, unshaven face abrading hers, she had just let go. Sido had unclasped her breasts from her blouse and sucked on them. It had been a strange sensation; one that Rupi wanted to stop, yet wished would continue. Finally, when Sido had pumped himself empty into her, his hand covering her mouth to suppress her screams of pain, Rupi had learnt that there were other kinds of work, too, that a wife was supposed to perform for her husband.

~

Someone or the other would come to see the new bride nearly every day. Putki and Sonamuni guided Rupi through the social niceties, refreshing her knowledge from the wedding day. At times, the naikay's widow and daughter-in-law visited and sat for a few glasses of haandi. They stared at Rupi with their eerie, rolling eyes.

One morning, Rupi—having finished sweeping the inside of the house—came out into the kulhi, broom in hand. Though their part of the village was yet to wake up, she could hear the rhythmic sound of rice being dehusked in a wooden dhinki in a house in the other kulhi. Dhaak dhaak dhaak dhaak. The sound reminded her of home and of her mother. Roosters crowed in the Kamar-kulhi. The naikay's daughter-in-law crept up silently.

'Sido-baahu,' she called out.

Rupi nearly dropped the broom in fright. 'Oh! Marak-ayo,' she blurted, 'it's you. I didn't see you coming.'

'You're sweeping the kulhi today? What about Sonamuni? Where is she? And your mother-in-law?'

'Oh! They are busy. I finished my work so I decided to help them.'

'How nice! Such a good bride you are. It is not even a month since your wedding and you've begun working so hard.'

Rupi only smiled.

'I haven't seen you properly,' the naikay's daughter-in-law said. 'You're always with Sonamuni or your mother-in-law. Let me look at you closely. Come, come close to me.'

Her eyes rolled, and Rupi found herself dropping her broom. It was magnetic, her summons. Rupi couldn't say anything and only one line repeated itself inside her head: Come, come close to me. Come, come close to me. Come, come close to me. Come, come close to me. Come, come close to me…

'Baahu!'

Rupi heard Sonamuni. Yet she glided towards the naikay's daughter-in-law. 'Baahu!' Sonamuni rushed up and shook Rupi's arm.

The trance broke. Rupi stopped and turned towards Sonamuni. The naikay's daughter-in-law slipped away silently.

'What happened, jhi?' Rupi asked Sonamuni.

Sonamuni said curtly, 'Come inside the house,' and pulled Rupi away.

What Sonamuni told Rupi was quite extraordinary, but as Rupi was herself from the forests of Tereldihi, and had grown up hearing such tales, the story did not shock her. The mysterious child in the naikay's garden, Sima-Bonga, the nightly meetings of women on the bank of the Kadamdihi stream, the rolling eyes—she had had some inkling of it all.

'They say Sima-Bonga was getting too expensive for the naikay,' Sonamuni said. 'All those sacrifices to feed the bad god. The naikay began losing his mind.'

Rupi listened attentively.

'I've seen the naikay's family for a long time,' Sonamuni continued. 'I've seen them change. His wife was a stout lady. She was older than both Khorda-dada and Putki-hili, but she was healthier. Such burly arms. I remember her arms. But Sima-Bonga took her health away. Her arms shrivelled and now she is all bone. Their son has not sired a child and the daughter-in-law is also a dahni. This is the end of their line. If such things don't kill a man, what will?'

'Did Sima-Bonga kill him, the naikay?' Rupi asked.

'Maybe. Sima-Bonga kills those who are unable to keep it sated and happy. The naikay was just found dead one morning. No disease, no fever, nothing. But you know one thing, baahu? Those who know about these things say that they noticed something peculiar about the naikay's corpse.'

'What did they notice?'

'His liver was missing! The space it should have occupied was empty.'

'His liver?'

'Yes!'

'Oh! That means...'

'That means he was devoured by a witch. Maybe his own wife...'

~

Two months later, Sido announced that he would take his wife to Nitra.

'I'm coming back on Thursday,' he told his wife. 'I've taken leave, we'll arrange our things. Tell me, you want to come with me?'

'Yes.' Rupi smiled. Sido took her in an embrace.

A few days before Rupi was to leave, a woman visited the

naikay's house. She was elegantly dressed in a pnaahnaar, the traditional four-piece ensemble worn by Santhal women. Her neck was adorned by a long silver necklace—tiny silver flowers connected in a chain. The woman's hair was oiled and neatly combed into a large bun. Despite her age, the woman had stuck a large, pink joba flower to one side of her bun. She presented quite a sight as she made her way into Kadamdihi.

The woman had a satchel hanging from her shoulder and an umbrella over her head. She went into the naikay's house, dumped her satchel and umbrella there, and quickly ran out and into Putki's house. Soon Putki and the woman were hugging each other and bawling like young children.

'Why did it take you so long to come, Reyar-Baha?' Putki asked between sobs.

'Tira and I were visiting relatives in Horoghutu,' Della said. 'When I came to know of your son's wedding, I came running.'

'It took you so long,' Putki said. 'It is unbelievable.'

'I wanted to come earlier. But I was caught up with my own work. My sons are in Namal. I heard about your son. How lucky he is; learned, working. You know, he works with a boy from our village, from our Horoghutu. His name is Bairam. His wife is from Jirapara, that village on the other side of the Chakuliya station. Her name is Gurubari. His family told me about your son. Bairam's family is not very happy with him or with his wife. So Gurubari hardly goes to Horoghutu. They're planning to settle down in Chakuliya. But that's none of our business, is it?'

Putki was weeping, snot coursing down her lips and chin.

'My Reyar-Baha,' Della said, 'I am not here to see my family. I have kept my bag in that house. I am afraid they will open my bag and do some magic to my things. But I am not worried. If something happens to me, I will not spare them. That woman is not my mother, she is just a witch. She ate my father up. And that barren sister-in-law of mine, she is being punished for her sins, for all the men and cattle she has killed. You know, Reyar-Baha, it was painful to hear about my own father's death. And my brother is completely bedridden now. I don't know what will become of him.'

They cried, Putki and Della, holding on to each another for full five minutes. After that, it was time for introductions and blessings. Sonamuni helped Rupi carry a lota of water and place it on the ground before Della's feet. She knelt before Della and bent to touch the ground with her forehead. Della grabbed her by the shoulders.

'No, no, baahu,' Della said holding her tight against her bosom. 'I do not need these formalities. You know, I used to be friends with your mother-in-law. What times we had! I will remember them till the day I die. You are my own, like my own blood. May you prosper, may you be happy always.'

'I am so sorry,' Putki said. 'I don't have my Sido with me now. He is in Nitra.'

'Oh! I wanted so much to see him,' Della sighed. 'I don't know if I'll ever see him. But I've seen your husband, and Doso. He looks just like his father.'

'Are you returning to Namal soon?' Putki asked.

'Yes, very soon.'

Nitra

Doso took Sido and Rupi to the Chakuliya Railway Station in a bullock cart. Rupi was travelling to Chakuliya after a long time. She peered out from under the dhacha which covered the cart and tried to refresh her memory. The tamarind tree by the road seemed to have grown denser, the banyan seemed to have put out a couple of new aerial roots, and the road itself seemed busier than before. A memorial, which had been built in the memory of a Marwari businessman, seemed more weather-beaten than ever. The memorial, built on the bank of a stream ritually used as a crematorium, was a hexagonal platform which could be reached by stairs. The domed roof of the platform was supported by six columns. There was an open space around the memorial and the entire place was enclosed within tall walls punctuated by an ornate gate. The open space inside once used to be a garden but had fallen into a state of disrepair. There were still some hibiscus and chiro-bosonto shrubs which the dead man's relatives had planted and tended to. However, no one visited anymore. The memorial had long lost its colour and the plaster, too, was flaking away. The outer walls were overgrown with tangled bougainvillea vines, whose pink bracts promised rest to travel-weary men and women. But everyone went there in groups and no one ever entered the premises alone or after sunset.

The first time Rupi had seen the memorial, she had fallen in love with it. Especially after she had been told of the ghost which roamed the place after sundown. On every journey, Rupi would stare hard at the memorial, trying to catch a glimpse of the ghost.

As Doso guided the bullocks and Sido dozed, Rupi stared at the memorial. She'd wanted to visit it one day and to explore the place. But now she was married and there was no way she could visit the memorial.

'Do you think this place is really haunted? It looks so grand,' she wanted to ask Sido. She almost reached out to wake him. But hearing him snore, she withdrew her hand and placed it on her lap. She did not peer out of the dhacha any more. Instead, she looked at the road and at the signs which heralded Chakuliya: the whitewashed building of a boys' school; a tall, watchtower-like house; the chimneys of the rice mill; the grove around a pond; the bullocks' dancing heads; and at Doso who shouted at the animals: Hee-ya! Hee-bey!

~

Looking out of the window of the morning passenger train, Rupi replayed all the events after her first meeting with Sido—when he had come with his parents, brother, uncles, aunts and cousins to see her at her parents' house—to her sitting in a train for the first time on the way to her husband's house in Nitra. She was dressed in a cotton sari. The sari, which had not been washed even once, was crisp with starch. The blouse she wore, too, was brand new and still bore the factory label somewhere between a breast and an armpit. She wore a slender but bold streak of sindoor which ran down the parting in her hair to her forehead. She was sure she looked like a diku, a non-Santhal.

'I am looking like a diku, yo,' she had said to Putki who was helping her to dress up.

'So what?' Putki had said. 'Can only dikus dress up well? Today we will show them how well-dressed a Santar bride can be.'

Sido did not speak to Rupi at all. It was as if he regretted his decision to take his wife to Nitra. But he was protective. He put his arms around her when the train pulled in. He was the first to climbed up into the bogey first and then silently pulled up Rupi and guided her to a vacant seat by the window. Doso then handed the bags and the trunk to Sido, who adjusted them under the berths and on the overhead luggage carriers. He did this in complete silence, with not even a word of farewell to Doso. However, as the train pulled out of the station, and familiar views began receding, Sido pointed to a huge red building by the railway tracks.

'There,' he said. 'That is the school I went to.'

His words brought Rupi out of her stupor. 'Which one? Show me,' she said. The building was on the other side of the tracks and Rupi got up to get a better look.

'Don't stand,' he said. 'It's still visible. There.' He pointed to the building again. 'That one.'

'Oh!' Rupi caught a fleeting glance before the building slipped out of sight. 'But there are no children.'

'The school starts at nine. It is only six-thirty now.'

'Oh.' Rupi nodded. Her eyes were still trying to grasp one final glimpse of the building.

'Such a lucky girl,' her relatives had said. 'Her husband went to school and is now a teacher.'

Rupi wanted to capture in her memory the image of that place which had made her husband and, in turn, herself, worthy of envy. She kept staring out of the window till Sido pointed to a pond beside a building with chimneys and a trident-shaped lightning conductor.

'There,' he said. 'You see that?'

'What?'

'There. It is right in front of your eyes. What is that?'

Rupi shook her head. It looked like a factory but she could not be sure.

'That is the rice mill,' Sido explained. 'My mother said she used to work there.'

Rupi nodded. Sonamuni had told her that story the day she had met Della, tempering the spicier parts with tame words. However, the story was still scandalous and Rupi had not been able to tell if she should laugh at her mother-in-law's adventures or keep blushing as befitted a new bride. And a question bothered her: Why did women like Putki and Della, who belonged to prosperous families, ever need to work in a factory? She wondered if her husband was aware of his mother's past. Rupi turned to take one last look at the rice mill.

For a long time afterwards, they did not speak. Rupi busied herself with looking at passing trees, cows, fields and forests; at the ruins of the huge aerodrome which the Allied Forces had built in the forest outside Chakuliya; at the wireless tower which the meteorological department had erected atop a hill in Muturkham village near the Kokpara Railway Station; and at the railway power substation in Dhalbhumgarh, near the overbridge of the highway built during the Sino-Indian war of 1962. Sido checked to see that their luggage was all there: the trunk under the seat, a leather suitcase on the berth above them and a satchel on his lap. In some time, a hawker came selling peanuts. Sido bought some and offered the packet to Rupi. She declined; she could not eat in front of strangers. She pulled her sari tightly around her; the fabric was stiff and Rupi, not being used to dressing up formally, was finding it tough to manage. Sido munched on the peanuts.

Rupi caught a glimpse of the chimneys soon after the train pulled out of the Ghatshila Railway Station. She was itching to ask Sido what the chimneys were for. This was her first journey outside of home and a new world was unfolding before her eyes. There were so many things she was seeing for the first time and she wanted to know about them all. But how could she ask? Would so much curiosity in a new bride be considered proper? What would her husband think? These thoughts kept her silent, and the silence soon became unbearable.

'That is the copper factory,' Sido told her, sensing the curiosity that was making her restless. 'They dig out copper from the earth and clean it here.'

'Dig out from the earth? How deep do they dig?'

Sido smiled. 'Very deep. Very, very deep. They dig several holes in the ground. Like wells. In Rakha, there are several places where they dig for copper.'

'Really?'

'Yes.'

Some twenty minutes after the train had pulled out of Galudihi Railway Station, it crossed a bridge. Dhokor dhokor dhokor dhokor. Below the bridge, Rupi could see vines under the glassy surface of the water, clusters of hyacinths growing along both its banks, and the rocks which stood regally midstream. Rupi was reminded again of her village. She pressed her face against the bars on the window and her eyes took note of every current, every hyacinth leaf.

When the train had crossed the bridge, she turned her curious eyes to Sido.

'Subarnarekha,' he said. 'That was the Subarnarekha River.'

'That was the Subarnarekha?' she asked, incredulous.

'Yes, you've heard about it, haven't you?'

She wished the train could move backwards. She wanted to

see the Subarnarekha again. The River of Gold. She had heard stories about it, about the gold nuggets in its bed. She stuck her face between the bars on the window, willing the train to retrace its tracks, willing the Subarnarekha to return.

'Come, we have to get down at the next station.' Sido pulled the trunk out from under the seat and carried it to the door. Rupi followed him, lugging the suitcase and the satchel.

Their stop, Rakha Mines, was a small, nondescript place. It was mostly plain, which rose into low hills towards the west. It was smaller than Chakuliya, Rupi noted. It was very silent and still, like air gone bad. The platform was just a small room on one side of the railway track.

'We will go to Nitra by that.' Sido pointed to a minibus parked on an elevation and indicated to Rupi to follow him. A board placed on the windshield of the bus read:

RAKHA MINES RAILWAY STATION TO MOSABONI MINES
(VIA JADUGORA—RAKHA MINES—KENDADIHI—SURDA)

The conductor threw their trunk and suitcase into the dusty boot. The minibus seemed to be the sole means of transport to the township which Rupi could see in the distance. The driver and the conductor were in no hurry to move even after the bus became crowded and oppressively hot. Rupi huddled in her seat, her right hand placed firmly on the seat next to her so that it could be reserved for Sido. He was standing outside the bus, furiously wiping the sweat off his forehead.

Finally, when the bus started its journey, it was overcrowded and listing to one side. Sido took some time to reach the seat which Rupi had reserved for him. He had such wide shoulders, he had to push everyone this way and that.

'It is very hot today,' he said.

She nodded.

'Just half an hour. We will be home soon.'

The bus rolled down the incline and away from the station towards the township that Rupi had seen. At a four-point crossing, Sido pointed out of a window on the other side.

'There,' he told Rupi. 'That way, there is a temple. A huge, ancient temple, of Maa Rankini. It is very famous.'

Rupi had heard the name of the goddess. She tried to peer out of the window but her view was blocked by a man standing in the aisle. She tried moving her head to see more clearly, but couldn't.

Sido smiled. 'Never mind,' he said.

The weather became cool once the bus entered the township. It was very beautiful, with trees on both sides of the road, eucalypti mostly. The road was good, too, well-maintained and tarred. Rupi had never travelled on a tarred road before. She looked at the houses; they were unlike any she had ever seen. They were in storeys, one above the other. Rows of clothes hung out to dry on the roofs. The bus stopped and a few people got out. She looked at Sido.

'Not here,' Sido said, and noticing the look on her face, explained, 'This place is called Jadugora. They dig for uranium here. The mine workers live in these houses.' He pointed to the block of flats. Rupi could only catch the name of the place and nothing else. Her husband had mentioned that something was mined here. What it was, she didn't know.

The bus rolled out of the township and entered a wooded stretch. There were more eucalypti here and also other trees. The road was still tarred but not as well kept as the one inside the township they'd passed. There were potholes on the road and the bus rumbled over them. However, there were people on the road. On foot, on bicycles. A little while later, Rupi saw shops and roadside tea stalls. They entered another township, one with a huge gate at its entrance.

'This is Rakha Mines,' Sido told Rupi. 'They dig for copper here. Remember? I told you.'

Copper was familiar, something Rupi could understand. She looked out of the window. The bus had stopped in front of huge gate. A signboard on it said:

HINDUSTAN COPPER LTD
(A GOVERNMENT OF INDIA ENTERPRISE)
WELCOME TO RAKHA COPPER PROJECT

She couldn't read. A few people got out, a few more got in, and the bus began its journey again.

The bus ran along the long boundary wall around the township. The wall was cracking in a number of places and the drain between the wall and the road was overgrown with cacti plants and putus shrubs. There were tall hills on the other side of the road. The hills had steep, rocky faces. Sido looked straight ahead, an urgent expression on his face, as if he wanted to spring up and run out of the bus. Rupi looked out of the window, at the forests and the fallows of a new, unfamiliar place. At one point, Sido raised his right hand and touched his forehead and chest with the index finger, paying obeisance to an invisible deity. Rupi was curious.

'Oh! It's that temple,' he said, pointing to a tall hill on the other side of the road. 'Siddheshwar, it is called. A Shiva temple. Very famous. This village is called Chapri.'

Rupi nodded her head and peered out of the window on the other side but couldn't see either the temple or the hill.

'You can't see it now,' Sido said. 'It's on the top of that hill, we just passed it. Each time I travel to Rakha, I see others bowing their heads. So I too got into this habit. Nitra is not very far now. Are you uncomfortable?'

Rupi shook her head.

Hansda Sowvendra Shekhar

The bus slowed down at a place where, Rupi saw, there was a huge field with two goalposts at both ends and a whitewashed building in front. Sido got up from his seat.

'Nitra!' the conductor called out.

'Yes,' Sido answered. He gestured to Rupi to follow him.

The bus stopped and they got down. The conductor took their luggage out of the boot and the bus lumbered off. Sido began taking stock of their luggage while Rupi stood rooted to the side of the road, breathing the alien air of an alien place, too dazed to know what to do.

Sido shook her. 'So, we're home. Do you like the place?'

She nodded her head, her eyes lowered.

'Come.' Sido lifted the trunk. 'Do you think you can carry the suitcase or should I do it?'

'No, I will,' Rupi said and lifted the suitcase.

'Come,' Sido said and she followed him.

They crossed the football ground and went past a building. It had a veranda and three rooms.

'This is where I work,' Sido told her. And Bairam-da, too.'

He placed the trunk on the ground so that his wife could stop to take a better look. Rupi placed the suitcase on the ground and looked at the building. The rooms were still locked. She looked up. There was a board at the top of the building on which some words were written in Devanagari.

PRATHAMIK VIDYALAYA, NITRA
STHAPIT 1957
GRAM: NITRA, JILA: SINGHBHUM
BIHAR

She couldn't read the board. She gazed at the wall before her and the locked doors. There was another board, this one hanging on the wall.

'There, see?' Sido pointed to the board. 'My name is written there.'

He climbed up to the veranda and pointed to a name on the board. SIDO BASKEY, it said in Devanagari.

'This is my name,' Sido said. He then pointed to a name written above his. BAIRAM TUDU, it read, in Devanagari again.

He smiled at Rupi. 'And this one is Bairam-da's name. This is a list of all those who work here. The staff of this school.'

Rupi could only nod her head. She was proud of the man she was married to, and was very happy, but she couldn't express that pride or happiness in words. I'm such a fool! she thought to herself, and looked longingly at her husband who grinned as he stepped down from the veranda.

'Come, let's not delay,' he said, picking up the trunk. 'The peon will be here soon to unlock the doors.'

They followed a dirt track behind the school and walking along an aaday between two fallows, entered a thicket. On the other side of the thicket, Rupi could see houses.

'There,' Sido said. 'That is the village.'

The men and women of the village stopped to look at the couple.

'Your bride, Sido-mastar?' a woman asked, taking a good look at Rupi. Though the woman looked kind, Rupi felt self-conscious and pulled the anchar of her sari around herself and inched closer to Sido.

'Yes, marak-ayo,' Sido replied, smiling.

'Go, go,' the woman said. 'The majhi's wife must be waiting. All she can talk about these days is you.' She stared at Rupi from head to toe. Rupi couldn't take her eyes off her.

They arrived at the majhi's house, which was bigger than the house of the majhi of Kadamdihi and far bigger than the house of the majhi of Tereldihi. Rupi scanned the house from one end to the other. There was a large byre on the leftmost end and a tall concrete pylon at the rightmost from which thick wires projected. The pylon, she assumed, went deep inside the ground and there was, she saw, another thick cable which started at the top of the pylon and went diagonally into the earth a few metres away. That is the earthing wire, Sido would explain to her later.

Nitra was one of the few villages which already had electricity. In Kadamdihi, they were still digging the earth to fix wooden pylons. And while Kadamdihi would soon have electricity, Tereldihi would remain unconnected for a long time.

Sido led Rupi through the open door.

'Look who's here,' a portly, dark woman exclaimed on seeing them enter. 'Come, come. Don't just stand there. We've been waiting for you.'

Sido and Rupi were brought indoors and seated on a pinda in the spacious racha. This courtyard was roomier than the one in Sido's house in Kadamdihi. Three young girls were drying paddy on a patiya. Two seemed to be about ten or twelve years old while the third was younger.

'We had a nice crop this year,' the fat woman said. 'What about you, baahu?' she asked Rupi. 'You people grow paddy in your village, don't you? Sido here says that your village is in a forest.'

'Umm...' Rupi said. She was not expecting questions.

'She's the majhi's wife,' Sido whispered to her. 'Talk to her, don't be shy.'

The majhi's wife turned to Sido and smiled. 'What are you whispering to your wife? No, no, no whispering now. Let me talk to her first. So, baahu,' she asked Rupi, 'what is the name of your village?'

Another woman, younger than the majhi's wife but older than Sido, arrived with a lota filled with water. She placed the lota on the ground before Sido's and Rupi's feet.

'Just look at me!' the majhi's wife said. 'I forgot all the formalities. I was in such a hurry to talk to your wife, Sido, that I forgot to receive you both.'

She walked to Sido and Rupi with her palms cupped. Sido joined his hands and bowed over her cupped palms. The majhi's wife uttered a blessing. 'May you live well. May you be happy always.'

She then brought her palms before Rupi who, hesitatingly, bowed her head.

'May you be happy always. What should I call you? You are like my younger sister. I'll call you mai. Look, mai, don't be shy. This is your home. Call me dai. Do you have an elder sister?'

Rupi shook her head.

'She's the eldest in her family,' Sido explained.

'You don't need to tell me that,' the majhi's wife said. 'My sister will. Why, mai,' she asked Rupi, 'won't you tell me about your family?'

'Yes,' Rupi mumbled, smiling shyly.

'Yes,' the majhi's wife said. 'That's good.'

The woman who had brought the lota of water cupped her palms before Sido. Sido bowed.

The woman kissed her palms and opened them over Sido's head blessing him, 'May you be happy always.' Then she stood before Rupi. As Rupi bowed, she could see that the woman's hands had tattoos etched just below the thumbs. They were small patterns, small enough to fit that part of the hand. Rupi could not make out what they were. Later, after she had settled in Nitra, she would see that they were identical patterns: a circle with a dot in the centre and lines radiating from the perimeter of the circle.

The woman kissed her palms but did not bless Rupi. Instead, she touched Rupi's chin with the thumb and index finger of her

Hansda Sowvendra Shekhar

right hand and raised her face upwards. She took a good look at Rupi's face but Rupi kept her eyes lowered.

'Very pretty,' the woman declared. 'Just like your dada told me. Sido, I missed your wedding, how unfortunate! But I am so happy that you brought her to live with all of us. Look, mai,' she said to Rupi, 'call me dai. I am also like your elder sister. I am Bairam-mastar's wife. My name is Gurubari.'

Sido had said so many good things about Bairam and Gurubari—Bairam-da this, Bairam-da that, Gurubari-hili this, Gurubari-hili that—that Rupi had become very curious about this couple. She looked up, smiling coyly, and froze.

Gurubari's eyes, Rupi saw, were much like those of the naikay's widow and daughter-in-law in Kadamdihi. Gurubari scanned Rupi from head to toe, from right to left, not pausing even once.

Rupi controlled her excitement and her apprehension. It could just be a coincidence. Sonamuni had painted such a macabre picture of the naikay's widow and daughter-in-law that Rupi had come to associate everyone who had rolling eyeballs with witchery. But her fear was justified. She had heard similar stories in her own village, about perfectly normal women who learnt this art out of thin air. After all, it took just two words and a half.

Rupi forced herself to act normally. It was just a coincidence, those rolling eyeballs, she reasoned to herself. Sido surely wouldn't speak well of a person who wasn't good. She smiled at Gurubari.

Bairam arrived with his arms spread wide. Sido got up and they embraced like long-separated brothers. Another man, as old as Bairam, dressed in a dirty shirt and trousers, with filthy, unkempt hair and tired eyes, followed him in. He embraced Sido, too. Sido would later tell Rupi that he was the master of the house, the majhi of Nitra.

'We have only just reached,' Sido said, pointing towards the majhi's wife, 'and baahu has already started interviewing my wife.'

'What did you say?' the majhi's wife asked in mock anger.

'Ah! That is bound to happen.' Gurubari held Rupi's hand. 'Come, mai, I'll show you your rooms.'

Gurubari took Rupi to their quarters after all the introductions had been completed. Of the three girls who were drying paddy in the racha, the older two were the majhi's daughters and the youngest was Gurubari's daughter. Her name was Purnima. She followed Gurubari and Rupi all over the house.

The majhi's house was bigger than Rupi had imagined. It was divided into two; both parts had separate doors. The majhi, his wife, their two daughters and maidservants lived in one half, while the other half—which had four rooms and was separated from the other half by a low wall with a small door—was given to the two Santhali teachers: Bairam and Sido. Bairam, with a wife and a daughter, occupied two rooms. Sido, single so far, had been occupying one room. The fourth room was being used by Gurubari as a store. There was a small open kitchen in a sheltered corner of the courtyard. Here, Gurubari cooked for her family as well as for Sido.

With Rupi's arrival, Sido would need one more room. Rupi, perhaps, would want to set up her own kitchen. The majhi's wife, who appeared to be a practical woman, suggested to Gurubari and Rupi that they sort out such matters among themselves. Rupi saw that as the majhi's wife suggested this, her face took on a strange expression. It was as if she had ventured the opinion against her wish, almost as if an inner urge had forcefully pushed it out of her. Rupi felt this, though she couldn't understand what such an urge could be.

The majhi, Rupi observed, was among the most prosperous

farmers of Nitra. The size of his house was evidence of his prosperity. He, however, was not only a farmer. He also worked at the mines in Rakha as a labourer, like many of the other Santhal men of the village. They worked in three shifts: A, B and C. The A, or the morning shift, was when the debris of the night's explosions was cleared. The B or the afternoon and evening shift was when minerals were sifted from the cleared debris. The C or the night shift was when dynamite was used to loosen ore. When Rupi first met the majhi he had just returned home from the C-shift. Which was why his clothes had been dirty and he had looked so tired when he had arrived.

Many women visited in the evening to see Sido-master's bride. The majhi's wife and Gurubari received them all. The majhi's wife sat everyone on pindas while Rupi and Gurubari sat on a cot. 'Now look at the good Sido-mastar's new bride. Isn't she beautiful? And she has told me that she too comes from a village which has hills like our Nitra does. I have already made her my younger sister; how many things we have in common!'

The women fussed over Rupi's fair complexion and her strong, healthy body. They asked her questions about Tereldihi, her family, Chakuliya, the train journey and about Sido. Rupi was shy, initially, but everyone was very friendly and kind. Rupi tried to locate the woman she had met in the morning, on their way from the railway station. She wasn't there.

The majhi's wife became so frank that she started telling Rupi about her father and his two mistresses. She giggled, and when somebody asked what secrets they were sharing with one another, the majhi's wife said saucily, 'E-na, they are very shameful secrets, you will all run away if you hear them,' and laughed so heartily that her whole body jiggled.

Sitting at a distance from the chatting women, Rupi caught a whiff of jasmine oil. When she turned around, she saw a very old woman in a white sari sharing her cot. The woman had rough white hair, of the texture of jute fibre, which she kept untied. It was her hair which gave off the fragrance of jasmine. Rupi wondered how she could have been so busy listening to gossip that she didn't hear the parkom creak when the woman took her seat.

'So you are Sido-mastar's wife?' the old woman asked Rupi. Her voice was shrill, like a goat's bleat.

'Yes,' Rupi said.

'Will you be staying in the other part of the house? With Bairam-mastar's family?'

'Yes.' Rupi's answers came as if in a trance.

'Have you been shown your rooms?'

'Yes.'

'How many rooms are you getting?'

'Two.'

'Oh! And how many rooms does Bairam-mastar's family have?'

'Two.'

'Are you sure?'

'Yes,' Rupi answered, her gaze fixed on the old woman's eyes.

'But you don't have a kitchen.'

'No. We don't have one now.'

'Gurubari has her own kitchen. Doesn't she?'

'Yes, she does.'

'That means the division of rooms has not been equal.'

'We'll have a kitchen, the majhi's wife said so.'

'Get your kitchen. A separate kitchen.'

'Who are you talking to?' Gurubari turned around to ask Rupi. This broke the spell. But when Rupi turned to face Gurubari, she had no idea what Gurubari was asking. The fragrance of jasmine oil vanished.

'What?' Rupi asked Gurubari. The other women were still chatting. It seemed as if no one had seen or heard Rupi talk to the old woman.

'What happened?' Gurubari asked. 'I heard you speaking to someone. Who were you talking to?'

'Here, she was right here,' Rupi stood up, flustered. 'An old woman, a very old woman.'

'What happened, Rupi-mai?' the majhi's wife asked. All the women were looking at Rupi now.

'Oh! Nothing,' Gurubari said, standing up. 'Rupi-mai wants to go to her room. We'll be right back.'

Gurubari ushered Rupi out of the gathering and into her own room, the room she slept in with her daughter.

'Who was it?' she asked Rupi. 'Tell me, which woman?'

Rupi became defensive. 'Dai, I'm telling the truth. She was there.'

'I know she was there.' Gurubari was motherly, calm and protective. 'Tell me who she was. Because I didn't see her, I need to know.'

Rupi tried to describe the woman. 'A woman, very old. Long hair…open…white…the fragrance of jasmine oil…'

Gurubari's face changed. Rupi couldn't tell precisely, but she thought it became worried and secretive.

'She must be an intruder,' she told Rupi. 'This village; all sorts of people come into it. And we are so close to the bajar: Rakha on one side, Mosaboni on the other, and Ghatshila so close, too. All sorts of vices are entering the villages. What to do? Thieves, all of them. What young what old. What were you two talking about, by the way?'

Now Gurubari was being defensive. Her speech had become disjointed and staccato, with frequent pauses. Rupi wondered why Gurubari should speak like this. Was she hiding something?

'She asked me about the rooms.' Rupi recounted her conversation with the old woman.

'Listen, mai,' Gurubari said conspiratorially. 'Let this matter remain between me and you. This is the matter of our house, yours and mine. There is no need to talk about it with anyone else, not even the majhi's wife. She'll be unduly worried. As it is, her house is so big and so difficult to manage. You understand? No need to worry her. Also, why should anyone else be concerned with how many rooms you've got and how many I've got? She must have been a thief, so she was asking about our rooms. And why have separate kitchens? Now we'll have the same kitchen. We'll cook together, like sisters. And my kitchen has two chulhas already. I will cook on one, you take the other. You understand, Rupi-mai?'

Rupi nodded. As Gurubari spoke, she was overcome by serenity and her doubts dissipated. Yes, she wouldn't say anything about this to anyone. They returned to the merry gathering as if nothing had happened.

Gurubari's Wish, Rupi's Word

The white-haired old woman was soon forgotten. She did not show herself to Rupi, nor did she try to steal anything, as Gurubari suspected she might. They never discussed her with anyone or amongst themselves. And Rupi did not set up a separate kitchen for herself. Gurubari just wouldn't hear of it. They prepared their meals together, ate together, and even did the dishes together.

Gurubari's persuasion was powerful. 'You're welcome to cook anything you wish to, mai,' she would say, 'this kitchen is yours, never be shy.'

Like honey dripping from a hive above one's head, a never-ending stream of sweetness, such were Gurubari's words. Rupi couldn't say no to her. And though she found this sweetness cloying at times, everyone was happy with the arrangements of the household. Gurubari ruled her house like a queen. Her husband, Bairam, was never cross with his wife and they seemed to be a lovely, ideal couple. After the suggestion which the majhi's wife had made about Gurubari and Rupi sorting out matters between themselves, she did not venture any more. As for the men, Sido was never concerned with matters concerning the house. Each evening, he sat with Bairam and the majhi and they drank to their hearts' content. The majhi's wife always kept at least two large pots of haandi in her kitchen. On some days, the majhi would bring Ingreji paura from the Rakha Mines market on his way back from work. He would then get his wife to roast some chicken for them and they would laugh, talk, eat and drink late into the night. When they went to bed, they would be in no state to discuss the house or its arrangements.

Rupi found it all rather strange. At home in Tereldihi, she had seen both her parents run the household together. It never seemed to her like any one of them had the upper hand. In Kadamdihi, too, her in-laws were like friends, equals, voicing their opinions, discussing them, at least talking to one another. Here in Nitra—especially in the house she was living in, for she hadn't had the opportunity to observe other people's houses so intimately—there was hardly any communication between the men and their wives. She had been expecting to talk with Sido about so many things—like how they had travelled together for the first time in a train—but in just a few months, everything changed.

'You want to return to Tereldihi?' Gurubari asked her one morning when they were shredding arak in the common kitchen. 'Why? Aren't you happy here?'

'No, it's not that,' Rupi said. 'I miss my parents.'

'Ah! That is but natural. I miss my family in Jirapara, too. But with your hoinhar's routine I wonder if I'll be able to go there soon. You see, even your hoinhar is not able to visit his family in Horoghutu.'

Gurubari told Rupi everything about her family. They were from Jirapara, a small village on the other side of the Chakuliya Railway Station. Her family was quite poor and her father supported them by sharecropping other people's fields. Gurubari had two sisters and no brothers. Because Jirapara was close to Chakuliya, and also because they had nothing much to do at home, Gurubari and her sisters—both of whom were now married—had attended government school. Though none of them had cleared even the middle-school exam, they were literate enough to sign their names in Devanagari and Bangla and read and write letters and papers in Hindi and Bangla. Gurubari's father was dead and her mother lived alone in Jirapara, looking after their farm and sometimes working in other people's fields or in the factories in Chakuliya. Gurubari also sent her some money now and then. Her marriage with Bairam had been a kondyel-nyapam. She had met Bairam at a pata and come to Horoghutu to live in his house and, having weathered his family's disapproval of their love affair, had become his wife.

'I want to settle down in Chakuliya when your hoinhar retires,' Gurubari told Rupi.

'Why, dai?' Rupi asked. 'Don't you want to return to Horoghutu? That is where the entire family is.'

'Durr…' Gurubari pouted. 'I don't think I can live there. After living in Nitra for all these years, so close to the bajar, I can't go back to fields and farms. Also, I don't know if your hoinhar's family will take me in.'

'Why do you think so, dai? You are a mother now.'

'That doesn't matter.' Gurubari sighed. 'I still remember how much they opposed our marriage. Now I just wish he would buy some land in Chakuliya and build a house there. Then we can live peacefully.'

How can she do this? How can she not live with her in-laws? Rupi thought. This will be like dividing the family. But she found herself sympathizing with her. She couldn't tell why. Was it Gurubari's honey-soaked voice? Or was it her situation? She wondered if Bairam was aware of her plans. But Bairam was either at school or drunk. He hardly ever spoke with his wife. How would he know?

Gurubari sighed one morning. 'If only I had a son. He would have looked after us when we grew old.'

'Don't worry, dai,' Rupi said to Gurubari. 'You will have a son one day. Purnima is just five.'

'When?' Gurubari asked, close to tears all at once.

Gurubari told Rupi about the boy she had lost before Purnima was born. Rupi began to understand Gurubari's urgent desire for a son. She could also see why, whenever Gurubari talked about children—any child, anyone's child, whether son or daughter—her eyes would glow. Her eyeballs would roll about endlessly and Rupi would be filled with pity for her.

'Rupi-mai, will you promise me one thing?' Gurubari asked as she poured water into Rupi's chala.

'What?' Rupi said, sifting the rice as the water ran through it.

'No, you give me your word first.'

'Yes,' Rupi said absent-mindedly, busy with the rice. 'What is it?'

'That you will give me your son.'

Startled, Rupi nearly dropped her chala. She looked up at Gurubari who was standing at the edge of the well.

'What, dai? I don't understand.'

Gurubari began to laugh. 'Rupi-mai, I just want you to give me your son when he is born.'

'But Gurubari-dai, I am yet to have a child.'

'You will soon have a child. I know.'

'Gurubari-dai, even you can have a son. There's still time.'

'No, if I don't have a son…'

'You will have one. Have faith.'

'And if I don't? Won't you lend me your son?'

'Dai, I don't have a…'

'You will have a son.'

'And if I have only one son?'

'You'll have more. Mark my words.'

'And then?' Rupi felt trapped.

Gurubari looked stern. 'You will give me your eldest,' she said.

The Son with Two Mothers

Gurubari-dai can tell the future, was what Rupi thought. For just weeks after their conversation, Rupi realized that something was not right with her monthlies. Also, there was a swelling in her abdomen.

Gurubari smiled when Rupi complained to her about missing her period. 'I knew it,' she said. 'So, how many months has it been since you last bled?'

'I don't know.' Rupi blushed and wrapped her arms around her body.

'Don't be shy,' Gurubari urged. 'Tell me.'

Rupi shook her head.

'I think it's four,' Gurubari guessed. 'Maybe five. You should go to a dhai-budhi.'

Sido jumped with joy when Gurubari told him of Rupi's pregnancy. That evening they roasted mutton and drank together—Sido, Bairam and the majhi. The next Saturday, which was two days later, Sido took Rupi back to Kadamdihi where she continued to work in the fields, despite her condition, and ended up delivering her first son in the middle of a rice paddy.

~

For the next eight months, Rupi stayed in Kadamdihi. Sido visited every weekend. All three of them—Bairam, Gurubari and Purnima—attended Jaipal's chhatiyar in Kadamdihi. Gurubari gifted the baby a pant-shirt set.

'How's Gurubari-dai? How is Purnima?' Rupi asked Sido on one of his visits.

'They're all fine,' Sido told her, taking fidgety Jaipal in his arms. 'They all send their love. They all look forward to your return.'

'When will we return?' Rupi asked. She did not know why she felt unable to stay away from Gurubari. And she didn't quite understand why Jaipal was always very well behaved whenever he wore the clothes which Gurubari had gifted.

'Soon,' Sido said. 'Are you ready to leave?'

'Yes,' Rupi replied enthusiastically.

~

In Nitra, Jaipal was blessed with the love of two mothers. And that came as a blessing for Rupi, too. For just weeks after her return she realized that she wasn't feeling strong any more. Was it the breastfeeding? The overexertion? The anxiety? She just couldn't understand.

She recounted the events of Jaipal's birth to everyone. It was the one thing the women wanted to hear about constantly: Gurubari, the majhi's wife, the servant girls, the women in the neighbourhood, everyone.

'It must have been a difficult time,' they told her.

'Maybe something happened then,' they guessed.

'A difficult delivery like this has its consequences,' they diagnosed.

'You'll be better,' they consoled her. 'It's just a matter of time.'

Rupi trusted their experience and waited for the day when she would feel healthy once again. For everything else, there was Gurubari. Always.

It was Gurubari who took Jaipal in her arms and rocked him to sleep. It was she who poured water on him from a jug as Rupi rubbed his supple limbs, and it was she who then massaged him with mustard oil. It was Gurubari who was always at hand to wipe his mouth and chin after Rupi had fed him. Whenever Rupi felt especially poorly, Jaipal even slept in Gurubari's room. There was, however, a difference between the ways in which Rupi cared for her son and how Gurubari cared for Rupi's child.

Rupi's care was natural and befitted a biological mother. Gurubari, however often seemed to forget that Jaipal wasn't her son but Rupi's. Most of her advice to Rupi on Jaipal's upbringing was followed by an assertion of how much more she knew about raising children than Rupi did. Rupi felt bad, and became gradually convinced that she didn't know enough about rearing a child.

A trip back to Kadamdihi was the only thing which could restore Rupi's belief in herself as a mother. Her health improved in her village and the chores of farming and herding proved welcome distractions from her enervation. No one judged her abilities in Kadamdihi; there, she was still the strongest woman around.

Rupi's resurging strength found good use in Kadamdihi. For Sido would take her back to the village whenever they needed extra hands. Rupi was a part of everything—planting during the months of Ashadh and Saan, harvesting in the month of Aghan and threshing during Posh.

'You need to get a bride now,' Sido would sometimes tell Doso. 'How long do you expect our mother to run the house and your hili to help with the farming?'

Doso would only grin. He had turned into a large man, much like his brother. He frequented patas, drank just like his mother, and many stories about his wildness did the rounds. Perhaps Sido had heard some of them, which was why he had cautioned his brother.

But Rupi would defend Doso. 'Oh! Why do you bother him?' she would say. 'You forget that finding a bride for him is your duty.' Turning to her brother-in-law, she would say, 'Doso, as long as I am around, you don't worry about who works and who doesn't.'

No one questioned Rupi's abilities in Kadamdihi, either as a mother or in the fields. It was only Gurubari who always demonstrated that she knew more than her.

Gurubari's imperiousness irked Rupi. Her mind would constantly go back to that day at the well when she had promised to give Gurubari her son. She wondered if Gurubari was making good on her promise. She couldn't pinpoint the nameless fear she felt. Worse, she couldn't talk about it with anyone, not with Putki, not with her mother in Tereldihi, and certainly not with her husband whose weekend visits had begun to seem like mere routine. And the more time she spent in Kadamdihi, the more Rupi longed for Nitra and their portion of the majhi's house.

But every time they returned, Rupi found that Gurubari's claim on Jaipal had increased. Her lethargy returned and, most of the time, she could not even feed Jaipal. It was Gurubari who fed and bathed him. It was she who washed his clothes along with Purnima's. And the lassitude Rupi felt was such that whether she liked it or not, she had to turn to Gurubari for assistance. As this went on, Rupi began to gradually accept that Gurubari was a better mother than she could ever be.

There was one other thing which was beginning to bother Rupi. At moments when her husband should have been with her, he was instead with Gurubari. He asked her concerned questions: 'How are you feeling?' 'Are you rested?' 'Do you need water?' 'Are you hungry?' And though she appreciated them, what she hated was what came after. 'Gurubari-hili will cook for us today.' 'If you need something you can call out to Gurubari-hili.' Rupi was unschooled, illiterate and a novice in the ways of the world. But she did understand that Sido belonged to her. And when she tried to make sense of the things which were happening to her, she could feel her head ache as if it would burst. So she lay quiet, trying not to think.

Rupi couldn't understand what her ill health had to do with Sido spending time alone with Gurubari. Sido should have been with Rupi. That was how it should have been. But all Rupi could see was that Gurubari would give money to Sido and he would obediently trot off to buy groceries and vegetables for her. Gurubari and Sido would also go out on the pretext of washing rice and vegetables and spend long hours at the well. And Bairam-master did not seem to mind.

Rupi—sick and nagged by the feeling that she was sharing her husband and son with another woman—kept to her rooms and walked over to Gurubari's side only when she had to cook in the common kitchen. She did not talk with other women. After some time, she built another chulha in her part of the house, but things didn't change. Somehow, she always found herself walking over to the common kitchen and cooking on one of the two chulhas there. Her own chulha was reserved for other chores like boiling dirty sheets and quilts.

~

Rupi had only two companions in Nitra. The majhi's wife, who came over to their side every now and then, and Gurubari, who was with her day and night. Among the outsiders, she would speak only with Romola.

Romola was a widow, not much older than Rupi, who lived

next door to them in Nitra. It was Romola's mother-in-law Rupi had seen when she first set foot in Nitra; the woman who had told her and Sido that the majhi's wife had been talking about them, the one who had looked at her very intently, but kindly, from head to toe. Romola had been married to the younger of the woman's two sons. The elder son was a farmer, while the younger had worked in the mines. After the younger son's death, his job had been given to his elder brother on grounds of compassion. Romola had no children. Rupi, curious, had tried to learn from Romola and her sister-in-law the cause of Romola's husband's death. But when they told her, she couldn't understand. Something had happened to the man, they said, which had left him unable to speak. And when he had tried to write what he wanted to say, his limbs had become paralysed. He died soon after. It seemed very mysterious, and Romola and her elder sister-in-law were not forthcoming, so Rupi decided to not pursue the matter.

After more than two years in Nitra, it did not matter how Romola's husband had died. She had more important things to attend to, like her son and her own failing health. Also, that white-haired old woman visited Rupi again, this time in a dream. And the dream, though Rupi couldn't tell for certain, surely had a purpose.

Rupi sees herself sitting outside the majhi's house. It is dusk. The sun has set behind the hills on the other side of the road. The tall rocks look like apparitions in the twilight. A light fog has fallen over the village, as if it were winter. Rupi looks around her and listens to the birds which are creating a cacophony in the dense arbour around the house. When the cold wind touches her ears, she shivers. It is then that she sees the white-haired old woman walking towards her.

The kulhi outside the majhi's house is deserted and so is the house, it seems. There is not a soul around; Rupi stands outside the house all alone. Out of fear or some other emotion, she can't move, her legs have turned to stone and she sweats despite the chill. The woman approaches, worry writ large on her face. It is as if she has come to warn Rupi of some danger, some calamity that has to be prevented at any cost.

'Your house,' the old woman says. 'It's still not right.'

What? Rupi wants to ask, but her words stick in her throat.

'What did I tell you?' the woman says in her goat-bleat voice. 'Don't you remember?'

Rupi woke up. Though she had dreamt of winter, of fog and chill, it was, in fact, the middle of a very hot summer. They were sleeping with their doors open. She herself was sweating. The sweat was real and her fear was real, too. Her legs still felt heavy and she had to move them to shrug off the terror. She ran her hand in the space between Sido and herself out of a motherly instinct to check on her son.

Jaipal was missing.

It took her less time than the blinking of an eye to sit up straight. Jaipal was two at the time; a toddler who ran about all day, spoke to strangers and ate on his own, but Rupi had not allowed him to venture out alone at night.

'You are to wake me up each time you need something,' she had told Jaipal very sternly. 'Under no circumstances are you to go out of the room alone at night. If I don't wake up, wake your father. But never go out alone at night.'

Jaipal, the warnings notwithstanding, was missing.

In a few moments, Rupi was up and out of bed. She had arranged her sari around her, tied her hair into a bun and rushed out of her room into the racha. It was a konami night, and the full moon was bright enough to see by, to help a lost traveller find his way home, or to warn thieves against breaking into a house. It was bright enough for Rupi to see that Jaipal was not in the racha. He wasn't in the corner where she usually took him out to urinate, nor was he in the common kitchen where they kept the drinking water. The door to the outside of the house was latched with a heavy hudka, as was the door to the portion of the house which the majhi's family occupied. There was no question of Jaipal having gone out of the house. The roof was too high for him to climb on to. Rupi felt her legs turn heavy again and suppressed the urge to scream with all her might. There was a burning sensation in her back and her stomach rumbled. She was about to enter the majhi family's part of the house when she noticed something odd. The room in which Gurubari slept with Purnima was illuminated. The glow of the harkane lantern was subdued by the bright moonlight but it was there. The door was shut, which was strange because it was so hot, they all slept with their doors open. Even Bairam's door was open; he had fallen asleep after an evening of drinking and she heard him snoring deeply. Why was Gurubari's door shut? What was she doing so late in the night? And why did she need to keep the door closed in such hot weather?

Perhaps Gurubari-dai knows where Jaipal is, Rupi thought, and walked towards Gurubari's room. Jaipal often slept with Gurubari and Purnima but Rupi always knew when he was with them. Usually, it was Gurubari who came to ask for Jaipal. This was the first time that the boy had gone missing.

Rupi pushed the door open. What she saw inside wasn't exactly alarming but it didn't seem normal, either. Before her was Jaipal, fast asleep on a mat. Gurubari was sitting before Jaipal, her back to the door. Her hair was open, uncombed, and in a wild tangle. There was no harkane lamp in sight, yet there was light. The lamp must be somewhere in a corner where I can't see it, thought Rupi, even though the glow in the room seemed to emanate from a crackling fire, not from a steady flame confined within the glass of a lamp.

Still, Rupi was relieved. 'Dai,' she called out to Gurubari.

There was no response.

She pushed the door further and called out again, 'Dai, when did Jaipal come here?'

'Why have you come?' Gurubari's voice was harsh. 'Do you think I will devour your child? Why have you come?'

Rupi stepped back in horror. The light went out. Rupi began to cry.

'What happened, mai?' Gurubari asked Rupi as she walked out of the room, her voice as kind and soft as ever.

Rupi couldn't stop shivering. Gurubari held her by the shoulders.

'What happened, Rupi-mai? Why are you crying?'

'Dai…dai.' Rupi's voice faltered. Her words were finding it hard to climb out of her throat and into her mouth. 'Jaipal… Jaipal…'

'Oh! Jaipal? Don't worry. He came to me some time ago and said he wanted to sleep here. Purnima is sleeping with her father so I let him. I wanted to tell you but I heard both Sido and you snoring and I did not want to disturb you.'

Snoring? I never snore, Rupi thought. And since when did Jaipal start leaving our room at night, all by himself, to sleep with Gurubari? But she said nothing.

Gurubari picked Jaipal up and handed him to Rupi. Rupi carried him back to her room as fast as she could.

Hansda Sowvendra Shekhar

A Whiff of Jasmine at Twilight

Jaipal was nearly three when Gurubari gave birth to a daughter, her second. She was named Pansurin. Purnima was eight then, and attended a school in Rakha with some of the other children of the village. Soon after, Rupi conceived her second son, Bishu. She did not go to Kadamdihi for her confinement. She didn't feel up to travelling. Throughout her pregnancy, Jaipal, together with Purnima and Pansurin, remained under Gurubari's care.

'You are spoiling him, dai,' Rupi would say as she lay on her bed, watching Gurubari breastfeed Pansurin and urge Jaipal to finish his bowl of khajari.

'Why do you say this?' Gurubari would ask. 'He is my son.'

Off-hand comments such as these would fill Rupi with dread. She would recall the promise she had been forced to make. But, she thought, why should Gurubari-hili not look after Jaipal while she prepared to have another child? It was Rupi's mind which raised doubts, and it was her mind which gave her solace. And when the questions became too torturous, she closed her eyes and tried to sleep. The white-haired old woman had not visited Rupi again. She hadn't yet told anyone about the dream or the vision she had seen in Gurubari's room. Not even Sido.

Sido would visit Kadamdihi on some weekends and would come back to Nitra on Monday mornings in a foul mood.

Doso, he found out, was carrying on with a woman from a village outside Chakuliya. The village was very near the rice mill in which Putki and Della once worked. The woman herself was said to be quite pretty, with smooth dark skin which looked like it had been burnished with mustard oil. But she belonged to the Sabar tribe, who were said to be so averse to civilization that they preferred to live on trees instead of proper houses. So primitive were the Sabars reputed to be that they apparently had no language and no religion. It was speculated that the Sabars were so useless that they had forgotten their language and religious beliefs over the years. They made do with a crude form of Bengali and worshipped Hindu deities. The government considered the Sabar an endangered tribe, gave them numerous concessions, and ran various programmes for their upliftment. One of the concessions granted to the Sabar was free healthcare in government hospitals. The Sabars, however, were mostly unaware of the benefits which they were entitled to. There was a residential school for Sabar boys in Muturkham village, at the foot of the hill upon which the wireless tower stood. Some newly admitted Sabar boys did not like their hostel. They jumped the tall boundary wall and ran back into the forest. Later they were found living with their families on the same trees from where the sarkaari babus had dragged them down. The Santhals had another name for the Sabars. They called them Kharya, which is another word for filthy.

There was a reason for such revulsion. There were many Sabars who had climbed off the trees and lived in mud houses in villages or in the houses the government built for them under various welfare schemes. Many Sabars went to schools and colleges, too. However, once Sabars had enough money or education, they forgot where they came from. In villages where Sabars lived together with the Santhals, the phutani, the attitude,

Hansda Sowvendra Shekhar

of the Sabars was such that they considered themselves to be better than the Santhals. It was little wonder, then, that when Doso began seeing the Sabar girl, it created much scandal.

Doso's Sabar girl worked in factories and at construction sites and lived with her parents. Doso was spending all his money buying things for her: clothes, jewellery, rice, vegetables. Everyone seemed to know about it and gossiped about the affair in hushed voices, so chances were that Khorda and Putki knew about it, too. But if they did, they said nothing.

'You cannot waste the family's money like this,' Sido had told Doso.

'What am I doing?' Doso had answered, avoiding his brother's eyes.

'It is high time you brought home a bride.'

'I will, when the time is right.'

'So, isn't the time right for you yet?'

'No.'

'And for everything else, the things you are doing, for which you cycle all the way to Chakuliya, for all that the time is always right?'

'I don't know what you mean.'

'Don't think that I don't know about what is going on between you and that Kharya girl,' Sido had finally said, unable to control himself.

Doso had looked at his brother for the first time during the conversation and had said evenly, 'I, too, know quite well what's cooking between you and Bairam-mastar's wife.'

This reply had silenced Sido.

But each weekend, the brothers continued to have heated exchanges.

'You are not a child any more,' Sido would caution Doso. 'All of this must stop. You are old enough, you know your responsibilities. You must get married.'

'At least I'm a bachelor,' Doso would say elliptically. 'What makes me sad is when married men with children make mistakes and scold others.'

Khorda was still active on the farm but old age was fast catching up with him. When he coughed it seemed as if he would hawk his very lungs out. Thick mucus made breathing difficult and he made gurgling sounds in his sleep. There was chronic pain in his joints. Putki was drinking more than ever. She was unable to brew haandi at home any more, so she went around the village seeking intoxication in other people's houses. Usually, it was the majhi's house. And after she had drunk enough, she would unload her bag of miseries.

'My sons are quarrelling every day,' she would cry. 'Doso is still seeing that Kharya girl. I don't know what to tell him.'

The women of the majhi house would try to console her. 'Putki-dai, he's a grown man. What will you possibly tell him? When he gets married, he'll understand.'

'And Sido? A father of two sons! What is he doing with that Bairam-mastar's wife? What?'

No one would say anything to this. Instead, they would top up Putki's glass hoping that she would fall asleep and spare them. And in her sleep, Putki would mumble, 'I knew this Bairam-mastar was not a good man. My Reyar-Baha had told me. She told me he's not on good terms with his family. But my son, my Sido, doesn't understand…'

'Like mother, like sons,' the women of the majhi house would jeer once Putki began snoring. 'Sido and Doso really are Putki's sons. There is no doubt about that.'

Elesewhere, death visited Putki's neighbours. The naikay's son, who had long been bedridden, died. No one checked his abdomen to see if his liver was in its appointed place, though everyone blamed his wife for his death. Some even blamed his mother.

~

In Nitra, Gurubari was as upbeat as ever.

'Mai,' she happily told Rupi one morning as they were filling their pitchers at the well, 'your hoinhar has found a plot of land near Chakuliya. We'll have our own house, finally.'

'That's very nice, dai.' Rupi said, trying to smile through her pallor.

'What's wrong?' Gurubari asked. 'You don't seem to be keeping well. Do you have fever?'

'No,' Rupi said. 'I am just feeling tired.'

'Now what's wrong with you?' Sido growled when Rupi told him that she wasn't feeling well. 'You were perfectly all right yesterday.'

Rupi said nothing.

Gurubari had to intervene later. 'Babu,' she told Sido, 'your wife doesn't seem to be keeping too well nowadays. Why don't you take her somewhere?'

Sido tried to shrug her off. 'It's nothing, hili. She's quite healthy. In Kadamdihi she does the work of three women. When I tell Doso to get married, she's the first to defend him. She says he'll marry whenever he feels like it. What can I say to a woman like this?'

Gurubari said, 'Whatever she says, she's the one who'll look after your house, raise your sons and cook your meals. Just look at her, she is not the Rupi of before.'

Gurubari's persuasion had an effect on Sido. He made enquiries and then took Rupi to a doctor in Rakha.

It was Rupi's first ever visit to a doctor. He was a young man, far younger than Sido; that she could tell. He talked to her in Bangla, for that was the only language she could speak—that too partly—besides Santhali. She was scared and the words refused to come. The doctor spoke softly, stressing each word, trying to make her feel comfortable.

'So, didi,' he asked, 'you have two children?'

Rupi nodded. Yes.

'How old are they?'

She looked at Sido.

He began, 'You see, daktar-babu...'

'Please.' The doctor lifted his hand off the table in Sido's direction. 'Let the patient answer. She can do it. Yes, didi,' he turned to face Rupi, 'how old did you say they are?'

'Chho bochhor du bochhor,' Rupi blurted.

'Huh?' The doctor couldn't understand what she had said. Rupi gulped. Sido was getting nervous.

No, the doctor had got it. 'Six and two, right?' he asked, looking at them both. 'Six and two?'

'Yes, yes.' Sido grinned in relief.

The doctor touched Rupi's chest and back with something which looked like a large coin connected to a black, snake-like tube. When Rupi looked up, she was amazed to see that the tube was connected to the doctor's ears. The doctor removed the coin from her chest and said she was well, though in a voice filled with doubt.

Then a man—who, Sido would later explain, was the doctor's compounder—took her into a cubicle where he punctured the tip of the ring finger of her left hand with a needle, wiped away the first drop of blood and took subsequent drops on separate glass slides, then gave her a moist, strong-smelling piece of cotton wool to place on the point of puncture.

Sido recounted the doctor's opinion to Gurubari when they were back in Nitra. 'The doctor said that she is all right. He said that perhaps she is not eating well and overexerting herself. I don't understand, how is she not eating well? She is eating well. No, hili?'

Gurubari smiled. 'Well, the doctors know more than we do,'

she said. 'Rupi-mai has to listen to him. Let her take the medicines which the doctor has prescribed for her. Let's see if they do her any good.'

In addition to the many medicines for fever and general weakness that the doctor had prescribed, there were capsules, tonics and powders which, he explained, would provide Rupi nutrition. Rupi was to take them every day and to continue even after she began to feel better.

The medicines seemed to work. On their subsequent visit, the doctor remarked that the patient looked healthier than before. They collected the reports—all of which were normal—and returned home promising the doctor that Rupi would continue taking the medicines. But most of the pills and tonics Rupi had been prescribed were hideous to taste. She put all of them on a shelf and forgot about them. In less than a week, she was back to lying on a cot almost all day.

'You look awful,' Romola said to her when they met next. 'What's happening to you?'

'Oh! I'm just feeling tired,' Rupi said, not wishing to speak. It took too much effort.

Romola looked at her closely. 'Is this just fatigue? This seems to be something else.'

'What?'

'I don't know.' Romola shook her head. 'Have you looked at your face in the mirror lately?' She smiled a slant half-smile. Maybe to cheer Rupi up, or to distract her from the mystery. 'You used to be so pretty, fairer than all of us. Now you have these scars on your face. See.'

Rupi grinned weakly.

'It must be age,' Romola said. 'Age steals our beauty, too. None of us are getting any younger.'

~

Lying in her room one afternoon, Rupi reflected on Romola's words. She had indeed changed, she could see it herself. Sido-baahu wasn't the Sido-baahu of old, the strongest woman in Kadamdihi. In fact, in Kadamdihi, her duties on the farm had become a burden. It surprised her that she had been married for only eight years. Eight years, and she was already becoming an invalid.

'What is it, baahu?' the older women of the house of the majhi of Kadamdihi would ask her. 'Isn't Sido giving you enough to eat?'

'What has happened to your face? You seem to be shrinking!'

'It is high time Doso got married,' they would all say to Putki. 'Sido's wife has to do everything. She manages two houses, one in Nitra and one here in Kadamdihi. She leaves her sons in someone else's care. All of this isn't easy.'

They were right. She was tired of it all. In Nitra, she was the one who told her husband what to get for the house and for the family. It was as if Sido's only job was to teach at his school and bring home the money. In Kadamdihi, even the smallest task, like buying new clothes for Khorda and Putki, and even Doso, fell to her. This ungrateful man can go see his Sabar girl but he can't buy his own clothes, she thought of Doso. Her brother-in-law who, until recently, had her full support, had begun to irritate her. The hostility between the brothers had rubbed off on Rupi. Rupi did what she could for Putki, though. She bought her saris and petticoats, and the all-important blouses, without which she would go walking through the village with her breasts hanging out. She tried to teach Putki manners, too.

'Yo, how much will you drink?' she asked Putki. 'And why do you have to go looking for haandi-paura in other people's houses?'

Putki pleaded with her. 'Let me drink, baahu. And they are

not other people. They are from our gushti. The majhi-gushti.'

Rupi protested. 'Whoever they may be, I don't like to see you tottering about looking for a glass of haandi, as if you can't make it here in our house. Bring me rice, bring me raanu roots and I'll brew you enough haandi for one whole year.'

Putki laughed.

'Don't laugh, yo,' Rupi said. 'This is not a joke. You're a mother of two grown men. And yet you go out to other people's houses and get drunk! Your sons may not find this embarrassing, but I do. And think about ba.'

'Sido's father has seen the worst of me,' Putki said, turning wistful. 'He won't mind. Ever.'

There was nothing more Rupi could say. Sonamuni-jhi's stories about her mother-in-law and her best friend returned to her mind from her store of memories. But now, she could neither laugh at those stories nor blush; they only made her hate Putki. Whatever respect she had for her had eroded away bit by bit.

One day in Nitra, Sido asked Rupi, 'What problem do you have performing these small tasks for your own house? You were always ready to do anything, why are you so irritable now?'

Rupi was distraught. Her own husband did not seem to notice what she was going through. But how could she expect him to after all the rumours she'd heard? After the pangs of insecurity she herself felt. What could she say about her husband? Especially after what she had seen one afternoon.

~

The afternoon had been a hot one and an excruciating headache threatened to crack Rupi's skull apart. Seeing her suffer, Gurubari made her sharbat: lemon juice, salt and sugar mixed in a glass of cool water.

'Drink this and sleep,' Gurubari said to Rupi, massaging her temples and forehead.

'Jaipal's father will come,' she told Gurubari, grateful for the massage and the cool drink. 'His lunch...'

'I'll give it to him. You don't worry.'

The assurance worked like a lullaby. Rupi slept a sound, deep sleep.

When she woke up, the room was dark and empty and she had lost her bearings. Her throat was parched. Though the sweetness of the sharbat was still on her tongue, her lips were dry. She could feel the heat coursing through her body even though the shut door kept the worst of it out. She longed for a sip of water but found herself unable to rise up.

'Jaipal, beta!' she called out. There was no answer.

'Bishu, beta!' she called out. There was still no answer.

She felt as if the pain inside her skull had thrown its roots outside and had taken her body in its grasp.

'Anyone? I am thirsty.'

No one responded. Rupi felt as if the pain would shatter her.

'Jaipal, Bishu,' she called out again, her voice a whisper. She began to weep.

In time, she saw through her tears a figure rising from the shadows in a far corner of the room.

But when Rupi called out, 'Bishu? Son?' there was no answer.

The figure came closer. From its long, untied hair, she could see that the figure was that of a woman's. The faint fragrance of jasmine oil reached Rupi. Before she could react, the woman opened the door. The glow of the setting sun came in a blinding flash. When Rupi looked around, she found herself alone.

The light also brought some energy. She felt strong enough to rise and walk out of the room for a glass of water. She turned on her side and stood up, then tottered towards the door.

There was no one in the house. The sun was on its way down but, since they were in summer, it would be some time before the sun set.

Had this been Kadamdihi, the non-Santhal housewives would have started preparing for the evening, lighting the dhuna and blowing the conches. Kaalsandhya, they called it; the in-between period between sunset and darkness. The time of the spirits. The Santhal housewives of Kadamdihi did not light dhuna and joss sticks, they did not blow conches in the kaalsandhya. In Nitra, which was populated solely by Santhals, she missed the uplifting fragrance of the dhuna which seemed to enter each pore of one's being and she missed the chorus of conches.

~

Other than the fact that noise aggravated it, Rupi did not know much else about her condition. And the doctor they were consulting, too, could not tell them anything useful. On three follow-up visits, he said the same thing.

'This doctor knows nothing,' Sido declared after the third visit. However, the doctor's medicines—with the same composition as the ones he'd prescribed the last time but sold under different brands—did make Rupi feel better. This time, she had not tossed them in the back of a shelf but had completed the regimen.

She had then reported to Gurubari, 'I'm feeling better, dai.'

Gurubari had only smiled sweetly.

When the meagre progress Rupi had made was reversed, Sido was livid. 'What is happening to you?' he asked.

Gurubari interceded again on Rupi's behalf. 'She needs treatment,' she said, 'why are you talking to her like this?'

They then went to Mosaboni, to a doctor who used to work at the mines' hospital there but had set up his own clinic after retirement.

'You have to cure her, daktar-saheb,' Sido said desperately.

The doctor prescribed another tall column of tablets, capsules, tonics, injections, tests and even an X-ray of the chest. The tests—and the X-ray—yielded nothing abnormal or alarming.

'Why, your wife is fine,' the doctor told Sido.

'But she is always sick,' Sido said, smiling obsequiously.

'It's in her mind, I believe,' the doctor said, sighing heavily. Rupi thought he was exasperated, for he was unable to understand her problem. She was also afraid that Sido might have offended him. 'She is sick because she thinks she is sick,' the doctor continued. 'All her tests, her blood pressure, temperature, pulse, heart rate, blood, urine, chest, abdomen, everything is normal. Everything seems all right. Tell me, though,' he asked Sido, 'does she lead a stressful life?'

'No.' Sido's eyes spread wide in amazement. Rupi couldn't understand what the doctor had asked though she understood the opinion he's ventured: that she was sick because she thought she was sick.

'I can't say what it is then, except that your wife is absolutely healthy,' the doctor said, exhaling decisively, lifting a glass paperweight off his desk and dropping it back, as if to indicate that he had expressed his opinion, the patient and her husband were free to either go by it or seek a second one.

'The doctors in Jhargram are better,' Sido grumbled in the bus on their way back home. 'Everybody from Kadamdihi goes there. In fact, everyone from Chakuliya goes there. No one comes to these useless doctors in Tata, Ghatshila and Mosaboni. These doctors, they haven't seen you writhing with a headache or lying down for hours because you were not feeling strong enough to get up.'

Rupi did not feel better. She found this doctor unpleasant. She thought he thought too highly of himself. The doctor in

Rakha had been good. He, at least, had a milder way of putting things.

'Did you hear what the doctor said?' Sido asked when they were home. 'It's all inside you.'

She said nothing. The journey had tired her and she could sense the illness returning.

'It's all in your mind,' Sido repeated. 'You are not sick. So stop behaving as if you are.'

He saw her writhing in agony, clutching at her head and her body; he saw her spread out on a parkom in the sun-soaked racha like a monitor lizard sprawled on a riverbank. Yet he did not believe her. And he would not believe her if she told him of that old woman—who smelt of jasmine oil—who was lurking somewhere in their room, like a spirit in the kaalsandhya, who had vanished as soon as the room filled up with light.

~

The racha before her was still. The door that opened into the majhi's part of the house was shut. The doors to both of Gurubari's rooms were shut. A solitary light bulb hung in front of the room in which Bairam slept. Sido did not have a connection from the electricity mains outside the majhi's house. They still used harkane lanterns and diba. Rupi would have to light them. But first, water.

She had walked across the racha to the common kitchen and poured herself a glass of water when she heard Gurubari's door being unlatched.

'Why, the door of our room is open,' she heard Sido say.

'And Rupi? Wasn't she sleeping?'

She saw them both, standing together outside Gurubari's room, before they noticed her. Gurubari was retying her sari and Sido was shirtless.

'Mai!' Gurubari couldn't hide her shock when they saw her. 'What... what are you doing? Are you feeling all right?'

'I was thirsty,' Rupi said, her voice betraying no emotion. 'I came out for a drink of water.'

Hansda Sowvendra Shekhar

Mohni Medicine

Rupi did not want a third child. As it was, it seemed to her that her two boys weren't really hers. Her firstborn, especially; Jaipal. Jaipal attended school in Rakha, but Rupi knew quite well what he was up to: he was travelling with his friends on the roofs of buses to gaayaans and patas, he was staying out late and failing his exams. He just pretended to be a student. As it was, she harboured no ambition of turning him into a scholar like his father. Sido too had no dream, no blueprint chalked out for his sons, though he himself was respected for his education. Other than being a schoolteacher, Sido was known for one other thing: he was a skilled rhymester who could play with words and create short verses and pithy aphorisms. This ability made him quite popular in Santhal cultural circles.

Maagh-bonga naase hisid-hisid hoy te
Likid-likid hilaw-ena bir, buru, naari, dare

In the delicate breeze of Maagh
The forests, hills, vines, trees sway

Organizers of patas, Baha and athletic meets came from near and far so that Sido-master could draft pamphlets for them or coin catchphrases for their posters.

De dela disom-pera
Hijud pe se raska bera

Dangadihi Panchami pata
saaw-te mit-nyida Santari gaayaan

Friends from near and far
Come all for a day of gaiety
At the Panchami pata
And a one-night Santhali gaayaan in Dangadihi

In return, each time a pata committee for which Sido-master had drafted posters and pamphlets had a gaayaan playing in the area, they very respectfully invited Sido-master, Bairam-master and the majhi of Nitra and their families to attend the opening night. Sido, Bairam and the majhi always attended; the majhi was, at times, accompanied by his wife. Rupi and Gurubari never went. Gurubari would say that she was too shy to sit among so many men; Rupi was too tired for any form of entertainment, even conversation.

Jaipal and his friends attended the events which Sido-master could not. He was a regular at most gaayaans, patas and sports meets. Bishu was the complete opposite of Jaipal. Jaipal craved company and excitement. Bishu sought solitude, a space to reflect upon life. Though Rupi never paid close attention to the fine differences in her sons' characters, she did occasionally become irritated by them.

'Why can't you sit in peace?' she would shout at Jaipal, angered by him constantly leaving the house without informing her or anyone. 'Why can't you be like Bishu?'

'I don't want to be like Bishu!' Jaipal would say, flaring at the comparison.

'I'm not giving you food today,' Rupi would say at times.

Jaipal would not reply and would simply raid Gurubari's pots and pans. Gurubari wouldn't mind. Instead, she would feed Jaipal lovingly.

Whenever Rupi expressed her apprehensions regarding their sons' future, Sido would grandly declare, 'They have my farms.'

After these two siblings, who were so unlike one another, came the baby of the family: Phuchu.

His conception, though, was unintended.

~

The ailment had destroyed intimacy between Sido and Rupi. Earlier, before Jaipal, before her enervation, they would move easily into each other's arms. But after she was struck down, Rupi could not bear the thought of sex.

But Sido had needed her one night and she, too, had needed him. The result of this union was Bishu, but the pregnancy had been unendurable. No more, no more, Rupi had sworn. Rupi often wondered if that was why Sido sought Gurubari. The thought made her feel incomplete. She hated herself.

Each night she went to sleep nursing this self-hate. Sometimes she would wake up in the middle of the night and watch her husband snore without a care in the world. She would feel like moving close to him, touching him. But the very thought of it would cause the inside of her forehead to throb. She would hate herself all over again. I can't carry myself straight, she would think, how can I bear my man on top of me?

Her man, in spite of how poorly she felt most of the time, did occasionally find his way to her. One night, he returned from a drinking session with Bairam and the majhi. Rupi's limbs were feeling numb, as if blood didn't run in them anymore. She was trying to sleep. Sido lay down next to her and embraced her from behind.

Sido didn't wear underwear at home and she could feel his hardness through his dhoti. A large man, his erection was in proportion with his size. Despite the numbness and the fatigue,

Rupi desired him. She lifted her sari and petticoat, spread her legs, and allowed him to heave himself on top of her. She took him all in: his alcohol breath; his unshaven cheeks which scored her face, neck and breasts; his teeth as they bit her cheeks and breasts; his saliva; his hands which squeezed her abdomen and her buttocks, and steadied her as he sank inside; pump-pump-pump-pump, she took his ejaculate in, all of it.

Rupi regretted being pregnant again, but she knew it was her fault. She would keep this child even if it killed her. And though there was no way for her to know it then, this pregnancy would reveal many things to her. During her pregnancy an incident took place which made her realize how vulnerable she and her family were. That incident, and what it revealed, stayed with Rupi all her life. More immediately, it compelled her to go to Kadamdihi for the birth of her third child.

~

Early one morning in the seventh month of her pregnancy, Rupi was woken by a pain in her stomach. Though she knew this wasn't the pain of premature birth, it was sharp enough for her to not ignore it.

She tiptoed around Sido—Jaipal and Bishu slept in the other room—and went out to the racha. The night was receding. It was the in-between hour of dawn and she could see a faint light in the sky. No one was up. All doors were closed: Gurubari's, Bairam's, as well as the door which opened into the majhi's side of the house. Though she was afraid of venturing out alone, the pain was becoming overwhelming. It would take her only a few minutes, she reasoned, and she wouldn't go off too far. Rupi walked briskly to the outside door, unlatched it, and stepped out. The kulhi was empty. She gently shut the door behind her and ran to some shrubs nearby.

Rupi lifted her sari and petticoat, squatted, and voided herself. The cramp eased. When she was completely relieved, she walked to the well where there was a tub of clean water and a broken aluminium mug. She washed herself, then used some ash to scrub her fingers and prepared to return. She adjusted her sari, tightened it around her waist, splashed some water on her face, wiped it with her anchar, and turned around to walk back to their room. Then, she froze.

Standing before the door was a man, taller than the door, almost as tall as the house itself. She could see only one side of him for he wasn't facing her. He was looking straight ahead, as if he was expecting someone or guarding the door. The man had long arms and legs and a stout, animal-like body. He seemed to be covered by the inky blackness of the recent night. Rupi wondered if going to the door would be wise.

No, it wouldn't. She turned around and ran to the shrubs among which she had recently shat and sat on her haunches. She couldn't see the man from there and she hoped that the man, too, couldn't see her. Blood rushed to her head and she felt like tearing her hair out. The baby she was carrying seemed to be getting heavier by the moment. She couldn't sit still, but she couldn't run into the kulhi screaming for help either. Never in her life had she been more afraid. Not even while giving birth in the middle of a rice paddy.

Rupi stood up slowly. Her head throbbed and her legs shivered. Stepping out of the foliage, she could see that a house stood behind her. She ran towards it as quickly as she could, supporting her wobbly abdomen at its base with both her hands, and entered Romola's kharai. She reached the back door and banged on it.

'I was about to tell you,' Romola said after Rupi had cried, composed herself and finished her story, 'how you are drying up like a tree around which an alakjari has twined, how big and healthy you used to be and how sick you have become, how you are losing the blood from your cheeks and taking on the colour of burnt firewood.'

Romola's mother-in-law and sister-in-law had looks of disapproval on their faces.

'She will die, dai,' Romola told her sister-in-law. 'If she doesn't know, she will die.'

'Tell me,' Rupi begged, shaking with fear. 'Please tell me. If it'll do me any good, please tell me.'

What Romola and her mother- and sister-in-law told her took Rupi's breath away.

~

The majhi once had a son and an idyllic family life: he had a regular job and also owned many acres, his wife stayed home and looked after the children and the housework, his children were happy, healthy and well-fed, and he had a retinue of servants to attend to his every beck and call. But under the idyll, unseen things lurked.

These things may be unseen, but in a Santhal village, everyone knows about them. To guard themselves, people insert leaves of the madar-gom tree under shirt collars or into the sleeves and pockets of their children's clothes, they put black dots of soot from the bottom of rice pots on the faces of their babies; they rub the nails of their hands together whenever they come across anyone they believe is involved in those unseen things; they do not let their bodies, clothes or food be touched by such people; they avoid eating and drinking at the house of such a person; and they pray to be spared.

It wasn't certain when and from where the majhi's wife acquired such power, but everyone knew that three of her aunts were infamous practitioners of dahni-bidya.

Before his marriage, no one warned the majhi's family about the mohni medicine: the concoction which is prepared from the pith of the banana tree. This compound is perfect for whoever wants to seduce or influence another. If a woman in love with an indifferent man feeds it to him, he will fall in love with her. If a man burning with vengeance feeds it to his enemy, that enemy will die a miserable death. The only trick is that the medicine must be mixed with the food of the victim. Everyone suspected that the majhi's aunts-in-law had added the mohni medicine to the food that was served to the majhi's family during his wedding. It was how they made their way into the majhi-gushti of Nitra. And to ensure that any procedures that they might have forgotten were also carried out, the eldest of the three aunts, a widow with no children, came to live with her niece.

This aunt was older than anyone in the village. And although she was a practitioner of dahni-bidya, she was the neatest, the most immaculate lady in all of Nitra. Her voice was shrill, like the bleating of a goat, but once she began speaking, everyone paused to listen. There was magic not only in her voice, but also in her gait and in her silver hair, which had the texture of jute fibres. It always remained open, like a stream cascading down high hills. She would comb it every day after rubbing it with jasmine-scented oil. The fragrance would waft through the entire village, casting a spell of its own.

Evil has a way of bringing together the like-minded. Gurubari became fast friends with the majhi's wife. The silver-haired aunt became a mother figure to both of them, in both their worlds: the social world of ordinary people and the world of women with special powers.

Together, they would lead other women to the copse of sarjom trees outside the village or to a secluded place in the fields. There they would all dance in the silent ecstasy that arose from the worship of their gods. The ecstacy would peak when their high god, the Bhaatu, would land in their midst, and they would make their offering. The morning after the gathering, the sacrifice would usually be found dead in bed. Some of these offerings would have died an easy death. Others, not as fortunate, would have writhed in pain or fever all night, their anxious families at a loss. The victim would mumble something about someone riding his chest; he would see the shadows of women slinking about in dark corners of the room. At times, the victim might even name the women: 'So-and-so's wife is hiding in that corner…' or 'So-and-so's mother is climbing on my chest, pull her off…'

After the victim was gone and the weeping and mourning done, the victim's family might enquire about 'so-and-so's' whereabouts at the time of death. The families of the 'so-and-so' women wouldn't, of course, say anything. The secret, though, always became public.

Evil though, however powerful it might become, has to fall on its face.

The majhi's wife had become a mother for the first time after almost a decade of marriage. By the time she had her third child—the pride of the house, a son—she was old and was beginning to find sitting on the ground difficult. Her joints ached, she suffered visions if she stood too long in the sun, and darkness soothed her. People of her village spoke in hushed tones about how sinners were not destined to relish the joys of motherhood. The two daughters and the son she had borne were her answers to everyone's accusations. But just as she had begun to think highly of herself, the Bhaatu fed on an extraordinary offering.

The majhi's wife was away one night, attending a gathering

with the silver-haired aunt, Gurubari, and some other women, when her son woke up, thirsty. He was burning in a fever. His sisters gave him water and cold compresses, but nothing worked. The servant women were sent out to find his mother.

The servants couldn't find her anywhere. They guessed where their mistress was, but remained silent.

When the majhi's wife returned, she found her son mumbling incoherently and staring fixedly at nothing. Her elation vanished as reality struck. She fell to her knees near her son's face.

'Yo… Yo…' The hapless boy was gasping.

'Babu! Babu!' the majhi's wife urged her son to speak.

The boy died a little while later, with his head on his mother's lap.

The blow was strong and, as a result, the majhi's wife was struck dumb for more than a month. But the nature of evil hardly ever changes. If people thought that the majhi's wife was distraught because of her son's death, they were wrong. She was shocked, no doubt, but she was more concerned about whom to blame for her son's death. She thought about when she had decided to offer her son to the Bhaatu and, more importantly, if she really had agreed to sacrifice her son. No, no, that can't be, she thought, someone else must responsible.

And while she obsessed about fixing blame, the rest of Nitra said with glee that she had it coming.

Her obsession got the better of the majhi's wife. When she couldn't convince herself that she wasn't the one who had promised her son to the Bhaatu, she began to look for someone she could blame. But who?

It had to be someone with knowledge as superior as hers. There had been five of them that night, she remembered. She was there, as was Bairam-master's wife, two other women from the village, and the aunt. The women were no match for the majhi's wife, nor was Gurubari, yet. In fact, only two women in all of Nitra could consume men and animals: the majhi's wife and her aunt. The others still had a lot to learn. There was only one person the majhi's wife could blame for her son's death: her powerful aunt.

The majhi and his wife threw their aunt out.

'Your mouths will rot!' the aunt shouted. 'Your house will burn!' she cursed. 'You are throwing me out for no fault of mine, don't I know? You have eaten your son, you yourself! You have killed him, and you are blaming me? You will never be forgiven!'

She left with her immaculate bearing and her jasmine-scented hair, and never returned. At least while she was still alive. When Rupi met her in Nitra for the first time, she had long been dead.

~

Romola said to Rupi, 'I think you should take it as a good sign that you are being visited by the spirit of the old aunt, that she is warning you. Though with all this dahni-bidya one can never be sure.'

'We were not as lucky as you,' Romola's mother-in-law mumbled.

'What?' Rupi asked. Romola looked the other way. Her sister-in-law gestured to her to leave the room.

Romola's mother-in-law began her tale. 'My younger son was returning from work one night. It was after ten. Half past ten, maybe. He was alone that night. He was on his bicycle.'

Rupi listened intently.

'He usually came the same way every day; through the thicket behind the school building.' Romola's mother-in-law was on the verge of tears. 'That night we don't know which way he came or what he saw or ate or did. He came in fast, furiously ringing his cycle bell and fell down in front of the house.'

She pointed towards their front door and broke down.

'We brought him inside,' Romola's sister-in-law continued. 'We found that he had lost his power of speech.'

Rupi's eyes welled with tears. Romola's mother-in-law was inconsolable.

'When he couldn't speak, he tried to write out what had happened to him,' Romola's sister-in-law said. 'We brought him a pen and a piece of paper and a harkane lantern.'

'What did he write?' Rupi asked.

'He couldn't.' Romola's sister-in-law too broke down. Her mother-in-law bawled.

'Yo, yo, don't, yo,' Romola's sister-in-law pacified her mother-in-law. 'He couldn't.' She turned towards Rupi. 'His limbs stopped working. They hung loose, as if lifeless.'

'What?' Rupi shrank back in horror and wrapped her arms around her body.

'Yes,' Romola's sister-in-law continued. 'His entire body was paralysed. We laid him on a parkom. He stayed like that for one whole day. We couldn't think of anything to do, we were so shocked. Everyone from the village came to see him. No one could suggest anything. Then someone suggested an ojha. I don't remember who. Soon after his brother left to fetch one, he started gasping and...'

She sobbed. By now Romola's mother-in-law had controlled herself and was breathing deeply.

'And?' Rupi asked, staring at them both.

Romola's sister-in-law laughed the heartbroken laugh of a sad person.

'And what? He left us.'

Rupi took a deep breath and lay back on a pile of kantha. She felt tired and sleepy. She now knew why no one from Romola's family mixed with the people from the majhi's house. Socially, the men spoke to each other but there was no intimate interaction, especially among the women. Never. Romola's mother-in-law had looked at Rupi with concern when she first arrived in Nitra, but when the majhi's wife and Gurubari had invited the women of the village to introduce them to Sido-master's wife, the women from Romola's family had not attended the gathering.

Rupi wanted to fall asleep here, in Romola's house.

By the time Rupi left, the village was waking up. It had been more than an hour since she had left her house. Romola accompanied her for a part of the way back.

'Listen,' Romola said to Rupi. 'I don't know if I should tell this to you.'

'What?'

'You had once mentioned that Bairam-mastar's wife and you share the same kitchen.'

'Yes. Why? We have separate chulhas though.'

'Well, the chulhas may be separate, but it is the same kitchen, right?'

'Y… yes.'

'I don't wish to accuse anyone, but how can you be sure she hasn't put anything in your food, something that you should never eat?'

~

Gurubari was sweeping the racha when Rupi walked in. 'Oh! There you are,' she said. 'Where were you?'

'I had gone out,' Rupi said.

'For so long?' Gurubari stood up straight and raised her eyebrows. 'Is everything all right?'

'Yes,' Rupi said and walked to her room.

As Gurubari watched Rupi walk to her room, the look of amazement on her face turned into a look of knowing.

~

'Why do you want to go and sit in Kadamdihi from now itself?' Sido asked Rupi.

'I want to go,' Rupi insisted.

'Now?'

'Yes.'

'Now? Have you gone mad? There are no trains now. There's one in the afternoon but I'll be at school then. Who's going to take you there?'

'I want to go…today.'

'Look, try to understand. You're not in good health. If you go to Kadamdihi, there is no one to look after you there. Yo won't be able to look after you, you'll start working in the kharai, the fields, everywhere, and again it'll be like how it was during Jaipal.'

'Take me to Kadamdihi,' Rupi pleaded. 'Take me. I don't want to stay here.'

Sido lost his temper. 'I told you once, don't you understand?'

~

Later, when they were alone in the kitchen, Gurubari asked Rupi, 'Why did babu shout at you?'

'I want to go to Kadamdihi,' Rupi said.

'Kadamdihi? All of a sudden? Why?'

'I'm not feeling safe here.'

'What happened?'

'I just want to go.'

'Fine.' Gurubari sighed. 'You go. First you taste this arak-kohra. Here.' She passed Rupi a bowl.

'No.' Rupi shivered.

'What happened?' Gurubari asked.

'I… I can't.'

'What happened?' Gurubari grabbed Rupi's hand. 'Look at me.'

Rupi turned her head towards Gurubari like she was a marionette and Gurubari held her strings.

'Now,' Gurubari said soothingly, 'tell me why you won't eat this arak-kohra.'

Rupi replied, looking into Gurubari's eyes, 'Romola said...'

'What did Romola say?'

'She said that I must not eat anything you give me.'

'Why?'

'She said you might put mohni medicine in it.'

'Is that so?'

'Yes.'

'When did she say this?'

'This morning.'

'When in the morning? When you went out and were delayed?'

'Yes.'

'Where did you speak to her?'

'In her house.'

'What made you go to her house so early in the morning?'

'I was afraid.'

'Of what?'

'Of that man.'

'Which man?'

'He was standing outside the front door. When I was returning, I saw him standing there.'

'What did he look like?'

'He was scary. He was huge and black and taller than this house.'

Gurubari smiled. 'Now, you eat this arak-kohra.'

Rupi licked the bowl clean.

The Mysterious Ailment of Rupi Baskey

Phuchu was born in Kadamdihi but, unlike Jaipal, he was delivered at home.

After Jaipal's delivery, Rupi had recovered quickly. Recovery after Bishu's birth had taken just a few weeks. Once Phuchu was born, however, Rupi remained in bed for one whole month, crippled by unbearable pain in her back and lower abdomen. She could just about venture out for ablutions. And when she did, Putki and Bishu had to take turns to keep an eye on her so that she didn't topple over when she squatted.

Rupi's departure from Nitra had been mediated by Gurubari. She had told Sido that sending Rupi back to Kadamdihi to deliver her third child would be a good idea.

Sido had not argued with Gurubari about Rupi's bad health. He had simply gone home to Kadamdihi one Saturday, informed his family of Rupi's desire to return to the family home to deliver her child, instructed Doso to be at the Chakuliya Railway Station with the bullock cart on the day of their arrival, and had then taken his wife to Kadamdihi three days later.

Bishu had gone with his mother while Jaipal stayed back. As they left, Gurubari had assured Rupi that she would take good care of Jaipal, that she would be his second mother. 'Return only when you are better,' she had said to Rupi. 'There is no hurry.'

143

All Rupi had been capable of saying was, 'I will.'

~

Rupi stayed in Kadamdihi for six years after Phuchu was born, never once returning to Nitra. Her health, however, showed only little improvement during that time. Earlier, a visit to Kadamdihi meant that Rupi could at least stand up and walk straight, perform ordinary tasks in the fields, milk the cows. This time Kadamdihi had no effect. Rupi could not recover enough strength to work in the fields. The most she could do was to sweep the racha, dice vegetables for meals, or weed the garden. Even these simple tasks would take so much out of her that she would be forced to lie down afterwards to recover.

Putki did most of the cooking. Once, Rupi had been put in charge of minding the rice boiling on the chulha. But she nodded off and nearly burned herself. Bishu's alertness saved her. He shook his mother awake. 'Yo, yo! Get up! Get up, yo. You'll burn yourself.'

Rupi got up, groggy and unmindful. She looked as if she hadn't slept for days even though she had taken an hour-long nap just before coming into the kitchen.

Sido was furious when he heard about this. 'Don't let my wife go into the kitchen!' he shouted at his mother. 'If something happens to her, I'll kill you.'

He vented the rest of his anger on his brother, though his words were indirect. 'Some people don't have a sense of responsibility,' he ranted. 'They expect their ageing mothers and sisters-in-law to do all the work when they can very well bring a wife to ease their burden.'

Doso heard Sido, but since he seldom responded to his brother's barbs—unless the attack was too vitriolic to be ignored—he remained silent.

'Some people can keep women outside the home but can't bring a one home,' Sido said.

This was vitriol enough. Doso said, 'Some people are such fools that they blame their mothers for the disease that ails their wives. They have been blinded by dahni-bidya.'

Sido stomped out.

Jaipal sometimes visited with his father. His arrival distressed Rupi more than it made her happy. All he had were complaints.

'What has happened to you, yo?' he'd say, 'You better don't cook for us. See how you've overcooked this rice? It's pulp! I was better off in Nitra. I came here for nothing.'

Bairam too came visiting, bringing happy news about his wife and daughters. Rupi got out of bed to receive him with a lota of water but went back once the formalities had been completed. Bairam never spoke to her directly—as his position was that of an elder brother-in-law—and spoke instead to Khorda and Putki, making only indirect references to Rupi. Rupi heard the conversation from the dark privacy of her room.

'Purnima and Pansurin have grown so tall, you all should see them. Their mother often asks about Sido's wife. She had wanted to come, you know, hopon-ayo,' he said to Putki.

'The boundary wall of our new house in Chakuliya has been completed. I have also got a well dug. The water was very close to the surface and the workers did not have to dig too deep. Now the foundation is being laid. The construction will start very soon.' This he said to no one in particular.

Rupi heard it all and didn't say anything. In time, she rocked herself to sleep.

Putki's drinking continued unabated. And after every session, she would bare her soul to the women of the house of the majhi. 'Why doesn't Sido understand?' she would lament. That Bairam-mastar's wife is the cause of all that is happening. How do I tell Sido? He won't listen at all.'

'Doso will bring doom upon all of us,' she would lament. 'Of all the women in this world, he found only that Kharya woman to fall in love with? Chhi!'

'This Bairam-mastar, he's not at all good. He must be aware of what is happening in that house and about baahu. But he is such a close friend of Sido's. Sido won't hear anything against him and his wife.'

Putki, like always, would eventually drink herself to sleep.

One woman would comment, 'Putki talks sense. Haandi and paura make people speak the truth.'

Another might say with scorn, 'Yes, she will talk sense now, now that our cremation grounds call out to her.'

~

Even though his family had become the talk of Kadamdihi, Khorda led a peaceful life, away from village gossip and the secret lives of his family members. He was happy with his grandsons, and raised them to the best of his ability. Khorda had always been an uncomplicated man, and his simplicity had only grown over the years. He had always been a farmer and, to him, there was no pleasure greater than seeing field after field of lush, green paddy flourish after a season of hard toil. After that, after having seen one's hard work rewarded, came the unmatched pleasure of playing with one's grandsons. Khorda regretted nothing.

Phuchu was growing up to be an inquisitive child who asked many questions. One day, he saw some men pasting posters on the walls of the houses in Kadamdihi. The posters were printed in green and carried the figure of the sun rising behind two hills, the rays radiating out of it in straight lines. There was also a black-and-white picture of a smiling man.

'Godoba!' Phuchu cried out to Khorda excitedly. 'Look! It's Surya Singh Besra. Godoba, do you know who he is?'

Hansda Sowvendra Shekhar

Surya Singh Besra was a famous man then, a self-appointed revolutionary. Even children knew his name. A young and charismatic Mahlay leader, Besra was the founder of the All Jharkhand Students' Union, more popularly known as AJSU. The AJSU believed that the old leaders of Jharkhand, those of the Jharkhand Party, had become ineffective while the newer ones, such as Shibu Soren of the Jharkhand Mukti Morcha, were pandering to the demands of non-Adivasi communities such as the Kurmi, the Soondi, Muslims and others, at the cost of the interest of the Adivasis and the Jharkhand issue, to remain in a position of power. The AJSU demanded a more radical stance. According to them, Jharkhand was only for Adivasis, not for non-Adivasis.

Despite their rhetoric and Besra's vision, the AJSU could achieve only two things. First, through the late 1980s, they kept the Chota Nagpur plateau part of then undivided Bihar nearly crippled with their Jharkhand bandhs. Second, they brainwashed young Adivasi men into believing that they had no future in education and should instead dive headlong into the struggle to create Jharkhand. The idea that Jharkhand would be reserved for Adivasis attracted many young Adivasi men to the AJSU. These young men even set fire to their educational certificates, thus putting their futures at stake, and jumped into the fray. It was on the strength of such staunch followers that Besra won the Bihar Assembly elections as an independent candidate. His symbol was the rising sun.

Though Khorda-haram did not concern himself with matters of politics anymore, he did occasionally reminisce about the past, the sacrifices of so many Adivasis, so that a separate state of Jharkhand would be created. How they had all voted so excitedly in the 1952 and 1957 Bihar Assembly elections and how the Jharkhand Party had won the Ghatshila–Baharagora seat both times. But then, there had been the humiliating merger of the Jharkhand Party with the Congress, and how Jaipal Singh of the Jharkhand Party faded into oblivion. Khorda wondered if the new parties were any good.

~

One Dasai, Khorda sat Phuchu on the crossbar of his bicycle, Bishu on the pannier rack behind him, and pedalled all the way to the outskirts of Chakuliya, beyond the railway station to where the Dashami fair was being held. A huge effigy of Raavan had been erected, with one huge head and nine much smaller heads. With straight, stalactite-like canines and two large eyes of unequal size, the effigy looked more comic than scary. But to a small child like Phuchu it was scary enough. When the firework arrow was shot at the effigy, there was a loud bang. This scared Phuchu so much that he grabbed Khorda's leg and climbed up on him, pleading to return home.

Once home, Phuchu was his merry self again. He recounted his evening at the Rabon-pura.

'Ay-budhi! Ay-budhi!' he told Putki. 'There was a huge bang and I was so scared I climbed up on godoba.'

They all laughed. It had been days, months, in fact, since Rupi had laughed so loud. Her sons gave her all her happiness, the sons who were with her. The son who wasn't with her, she had given away. She had been true to her word.

Comparing Mysteries

Rupi returned to Nitra when Phuchu was six. Jaipal was almost a young man by then. All of twelve, he had grown a faint moustache which he took great pride in. He dressed up like grown-up men, in full trousers and shirts, unlike Sido who, at twelve, had worn shorts. All of Jaipal's friends were older boys from Nitra, Rakha and nearby villages. They roamed about in a group and Jaipal often came home late. Rupi had almost given up on him. Though, in one corner of her heart, she still nursed the hope that her son would return to her one day. She still hoped that Gurubari would go away with Bairam and their two daughters, and she would have Sido and all her sons to herself. The corner of her heart where this feeling arose was where it remained, an intolerable irritant.

After only a week in Nitra, Rupi found herself in bed again.

~

The six-year stay in Kadamdihi had restored only a little of Rupi's health. Even a visit to yet another doctor in Jhargram had yielded little. Rupi had gone along with Sido on one of his weekly visits.

The doctor was very popular. Many patients crowded his waiting room, some of them from villages around Chakuliya.

'Aren't you Sido-mastar?' a man asked Sido. 'From Kadamdihi village?'

149

'Yes, I am.'

'Oh! That's so nice. My parents knew your grandfather, Somai-haram.' The man laughed, pleased at having met Somai-haram's grandson, and kept introducing himself and everyone in his family—who were not there at the doctor's clinic, of course—to an amused Sido.

The doctor was a small man who did not look like a doctor at all. He looked plain and had he not been dressed in a formal shirt and trousers, he would have surely resembled one of his rural patients. He had a very gentle manner of speaking and was almost inaudible.

'Hyan? Hyan?' Rupi had to interrupt him many times during the history-taking. He remained unfazed though, and was very patient.

Needless to say, he, too, was unable to find anything wrong with Rupi. But he had a very tactful way of presenting his findings to her and to Sido.

'You see, this is natural,' he said gently. 'There's age, there's all that hard work you have to do. But it is nothing that cannot be cured.'

Sido was thoroughly impressed. Rupi, too, felt better after the visit.

Sido asked Rupi on their journey back to Chakuliya by the down train. 'Why, didn't I tell you he's a good doctor?'

'Yes.' Rupi, who had been looking out of the window, turned towards him and then turned back to look outside.

After the visit to Jhargram, Rupi could sweep the racha, even the huge kharai. She could sit in front of the chulha without being lulled to sleep by the heat. She could draw buckets full of water from the well. She could hold a water-filled pitcher in the crook of her arm and lug it into the kitchen. She also went to the fields and joined in, though everyone who saw her said that she needed more time to recover.

The women doing the transplanting asked, 'Sido-baahu, do you think you can manage it?'

'Yes,' Rupi said. Though the doctor's medicines had improved her health, Rupi's cheeks were yet to fill out.

'Look,' one of the women urged, 'if you're not feeling well, you need not come with us.'

'Yes, you can always sit there on the aaday, there under that kowha tree, and watch us work. You need not come into the mud and slush with us,' said another.

'No, I will. Nothing will happen to me.'

She waded into the slush, tired quickly, and sat on the aaday. But she had atleast made a start.

It could be that the positive vibes around her in Kadamdihi had had an effect. It could also be that the medicines prescribed to her by the doctor in Jhargram had done their job. Whatever the case, Rupi kept visiting the fields every day throughout the farming season.

~

In Nitra, Rupi's enthusiasm sank like a bar of soap would in a pond. After she finished the course of medicines prescribed by the doctor in Jhargram, there was no need to go to him again. And it would take very determined persuasion to get Sido to take Rupi to a doctor in Rakha, Mosaboni or Ghatshila. Rupi thus spent most of her waking hours in bed.

In Nitra, the silver-haired aunt returned to Rupi's dreams. She would arrive with purpose, as if she wanted to tell Rupi something. But each time, Rupi woke up before she could say anything.

She also seldom got the chance to speak intimately with Romola. Every time Romola and Gurubari crossed paths, Gurubari would look at Romola with hostility, or so Rupi thought. Romola remained undaunted, though. She was still a close friend of Rupi's, someone who cared. Whenever Rupi would walk back from the well and meet Romola on the way, she would smile benignly and say, 'See, you still look awful.'

Rupi, like a dog trained to retrieve quarry for its master, would report each word to Gurubari.

Gurubari would say sharply, 'Let people say whatever they want to say. You don't pay attention to them. I know very well when you look healthy and when not. Why, the doctors' medicines have worked. There is no reason for you to listen to all and sundry.'

Rupi did not know how to respond.

'All of it is rubbish,' Gurubari would say to Rupi. 'There are no old aunts.'

'But I see her in my dreams,' Rupi would protest. 'I told you about her. Remember? About the woman sitting with me on the parkom?'

'There is no such woman. Don't tell these things to anyone or they will think you are going mad. Who knows, they may even accuse you of knowing things you aren't supposed to know.'

Rupi would shake with fear. She did not want to be called a witch.

The recurring dreams of the old aunt, and having to keep everything to herself for fear of being misunderstood made Rupi even more miserable. When she next visited Kadamdihi, to see her ailing father-in-law, the village buzzed with murmurs about her failing health.

'This is no age to look like this.'

'Look at Khorda. It's only now that he has fallen ill.'

'And Putki? She drinks so much, lives on leftover rice and salt, and is still so healthy. What has happened to Sido-baahu?'

'What has happened? It's that Gurubari; she is feeding off Sido-baahu.'

'Have you heard? Bairam-mastar is planning to live separately from his family in Horoghutu.'

'Is that so?'

'Yes, he has sold his share of land and has bought a plot near Chakuliya. He is building a house there.'

'Oh! That, too, must be Gurubari's doing.'

'Why doesn't Sido understand?'

'What is happening to your wife?' a man asked Sido.

He was as perplexed as everyone else. 'What do I tell you?' he said, 'she is fine one day and the next she must lie down all day.'

'Haven't you taken her to a doctor?'

Sido bristled. 'Haven't I? We've been to three doctors so far. In Rakha and in Mosaboni. I took her to one in Jhargram as well. Everyone said she is fine. There's nothing wrong with her.'

Nervous about stating what should have been obvious to Sido, and wary of his short temper, the man asked haltingly, 'Have you er…thought of other possibilities?'

'What possibilities?' Sido asked.

'An evil eye, perhaps…' The suggester paused for a moment before rushing on, 'You live in a village. You never know, in a village…'

Sido cut the man short. 'What do want to say? That some dahni is responsible for my wife's bad health? Is that what you want to suggest?'

'No, I wasn't saying that…' The suggester began before Sido interrupted again, this time in anger.

'Look! My wife's health is no one's business. She was sick and I took her to a doctor. I did not take her to an ojha, the way many of you would have done with your wives. I am not a fool like you all are.'

No one discussed the matter further with Sido. Once Khorda felt better, the couple returned to Nitra where Rupi once again became bedridden.

~

Unwilling to take her to another doctor, Sido decided to try alternative medicine. The first person he took Rupi to was a man who lived in Jadugora, reputed to cure diseases with the help of roots, resin, fruits, seeds and herbs he collected from the forest.

The herbalist examined Rupi's hand for a long while, keeping his fingertips on her pulse. He was not an old man though he looked older than his years. He was extremely thin and his clothes flapped about his body. He wore very thick glasses which he had bound to his face with thin twine. The glasses kept slipping down the bridge of his nose and he kept pushing them into place.

'I see bad air,' he mumbled.

Sido nodded, even though he hadn't clearly heard what the herbalist had said. Rupi sat stolidly, like she had through all her earlier appointments with healers.

The herbalist gave Rupi some powder in a small paper pouch. He claimed that it had been ground from the the root of a tree which grew on some faraway mountain. Sido did not ask which tree it was or which mountain it grew on. He just paid and they left.

~

As Rupi took steps to improve her health, Khorda died. In his final throes, he saw a vision.

'There are two of them,' Khorda muttered in those in-between moments between living and dying, those moments of revelation, of realization.

When Putki saw him slipping away, she called out hysterically, 'Doso! Doso! Where are you? Look at what is happening to your father!'

Doso ran up to the door and stood there, groggy from sleep, for it was quite early in the morning.

'I can't...breeeathe.' Khorda's words were stretched, as if they were being squeezed out from him.

'What?' Putki asked, bringing her ear close to her husband's mouth. 'What did you say?'

'My chest... They're standing on my chest...'

'Who is standing on your chest?'

Doso knelt beside his father. 'Who? Who is standing where?'

'Those two.' Khorda said, and after jerking his head violently from side to side, exhaled his last breath.

When Sido and Rupi arrived in Kadamdihi with their sons for Khorda's cremation and the bhaadaan rituals, the air was rife with conjecture about what Khorda must have seen in the moments before he died.

'What was it Putki said that Khorda muttered before his death?'

'Something about two people. He said they were standing on his chest.'

'Oh! So did he say that he felt suffocated because of two people standing on his chest?'

'Something like that. '

'Do you know who those two people were?'

'No. He died before he could say.'

'Do you still need Khorda to tell you who those two were? Can't you guess?'

'No. Who?'

'The naikay's widow and daughter-in-law, of course.'

'Oh! So was Khorda-haram really devoured?'

'Certainly. And did you see Sido-baahu?'

'Yes, she looks awful.'

'Poor woman! She is also going the way of her father-in-law.'

'That's true. It's that Gurubari. Why doesn't Sido see it? And why is Rupi not protesting?'

'I think that Gurubari has fed them all something.'

'You mean some kind of mohni medicine?'

'Certainly. Can't you see how angry Sido gets when we try to suggest to him that his wife's infirmity is not an ailment? That it is something else?'

'Gurubari comes from a very poor family. Someone told me her mother too practised these bad things. She'd do anything to drive Rupi out of Sido's life and take her place. Don't you see how she's taken Bairam-mastar away from his family? And she's turned Sido's sons into her own property.'

'Jaipal. Just look at Jaipal. He hardly thinks Rupi is his mother. He's never with her. He's always in Nitra with that Gurubari.'

'That's true. We can only hope Rupi doesn't die like Khorda. Imagine being suffocated to death!'

Not content with merely comparing the circumstances of Khorda's death with the circumstances surrounding Rupi's infirmity, a few zealous and concerned members of the majhi-gushti of Kadamdihi also carried out a covert operation to determine the cause of Khorda's death. The ritual was called the soonoom-paanjaa and was carried out by an ojha who agreed to perform it in return for some paura and meat.

The ojha took a few drops of ordinary mustard oil—soonoom—on a jackfruit leaf and mumbled his montros to begin the process of the paanjaa—the search.

'Did you say he mentioned two people standing on his chest?' he asked.

'Yes, yes.'

The ojha mumbled a few more montros and looked upwards. His irises had rolled up into his skull and all his clients could see were the whites of his eyes. He was sitting with his left heel pressed under his left buttock and his right knee bent, which is the proper pose to be taken when offering prayers and sacrifices to the deities. His head rolled as if on a pivot.

'Did—the—man—say—that—there—were—two—women—standing—on—his—chest?' The ojha asked in a sing-song voice.

The clients exchanged knowing looks with one another. Then, one man responded, 'No.'

The ojha continued. 'There—were—two—women. Two—women—were—riding—his—chest. They—devoured—him.'

The clients looked at each other. The oldest man in the group asked: 'Who were the two women?'

'One—old—woman. Very—old. Another—younger—than—the—first—woman. They—lived—very—close—to—the—dead—man. They—still—do.'

There was a long moment of silence.

Then, the oldest man in the group broke the spell and asked, 'Is that all, gomkay?'

'That's—all.'

The ojha's head stopped rolling and he became normal once more. Even though no one had been named, there was no doubt. It was the naikay's widow and his daughter-in-law who were responsible for Khorda-haram's death.

The younger men of the gushti wanted revenge. 'Such women are a disgrace,' they said. 'Should we allow them to do as they please?'

But the older members of the gushti were circumspect. 'There is no use fighting back,' they advised. 'This will only spoil relations between majhi-gushti and the naikay-gushti. Those who do bad will find bad. See how the naikay died. And his son? He's been left without an heir. The naikay's widow is old, and will soon die. Without her, her daughter-in-law won't be able to do anything. Leave them alone.'

As if fulfilling this prophecy, the naikay's widow died soon after.

When Khorda-haram died, the last custodian of Kadamdihi's morality was lost. His death affected the way in which the Baha and Maak-Moray festivals were organized that year. Earlier, both festivals would be organized in spring. But with Khorda-haram gone, and with other elders of the village uninterested in presiding over the arrangements, Baha was held in the spring that year, and Maak-Moray two months later, in the burning heat of summer. Gradually, the people of Kadamdihi stopped celebrating Maak-Moray altogether. Another family of the naikay-gushti, the new naikay family of Kadamdihi, had found the Sima-Bonga; they didn't concern themselves with the good gods. All religious functions to them were just perfunctory. Others were just indifferent. In Kadamdihi, faith slipped into crisis.

The Wife's Revenge

Doso met Dulari at a pata near Chakuliya. She was a thin woman with a flat chest and backside. She had a small mouth with a pair of large buck teeth. She dressed plainly, too. She wasn't the sort of woman a man like Doso would have normally fallen for. His Kharya lover was far more attractive.

On most days, Doso would drink his fill and leave which ever pata he was in at the time and head to his lover's house. After spending the night there he would return home in the morning, refreshed and entertained. The day he met Dulari, though, Dose left the pata and came home. He thumped the door loudly, waking his mother.

Putki was used to her son coming home drunk. But he knocked gently each time, a knock Putki had grown so used to that she rose from the deepest slumber upon hearing it. She wasn't prepared for the thumping Doso gave the door that night. Nor did she expect the tirade that followed.

'Marriage, marriage, marriage! My marriage is all you have in your mind, eh, yo?' he asked as he stepped inside the house and flung his bicycle against the wall of the byre.

'What are you saying, son?' Putki asked. 'Come in. Have you eaten?'

'What am I saying?' Doso growled. 'You are asking me what *I* am saying? As if you don't already know? As if you haven't said it enough times already, Dada and you?'

Putki now understood what all this was about. But she wasn't the one who was insisting that Doso get married, Sido was.

Putki's only fault was that she occasionally took her elder son's side, Doso had surely heard stories of her wild youth. Perhaps he resented being lectured to by such a woman, even though she was his mother. Whatever the case may be, the dam burst on the night Doso met Dulari.

'You will tell me about marriage? You?' Doso hissed into Putki's face and for once—she later told the women of the majhi's house—she hated the stench of alcohol.

'He was so drunk and angry,' she told the women, 'that he seemed to have forgotten that I am his mother.'

Doso continued his tirade. 'And that brother of mine, he talks about my woman when he himself keeps a woman outside marriage.'

'He said such dirty things about Sido, I can't even recount them,' Putki said.

Doso ended with this announcement: 'To make you both happy, I have found a woman for myself. I am going to bring her home. It doesn't matter whether you approve of her or not. She will be my wife.'

Two weeks later, Dulari arrived in Kadamdihi.

Putki said to the women in the majhi's house, 'I was so scared that he would bring home that Kharya girl. Thankfully, at least the woman is Santar. But for what sins of mine am I being punished? This woman, Dulari is her name, is nothing compared to Sido's wife. Oh! This is what happens when sons bring home wives and parents can only watch and do nothing.'

On one of his weekend visits, Sido organized a simple sindradaan for his brother and his bride. Once the formalities were completed, the bride price was sent to Dulari's family. All this while, everybody in Putki's family remained unaware of Dulari's origins, although all of Kadamdihi knew of Dulari's family and her village.

Dulari belonged to a poor family from a village near Chakuliya. Her father worked on other people's farms and at construction sites and at mills in the off season. She was the youngest of five children. She had three sisters and one brother, the brother was the eldest of the five.

Putki lamented her fate at the majhi's house. 'She's not the kind of woman I wanted for a daughter-in-law.'

The women sniggered behind her back. They whispered to each other, 'Now she'll know, this Putki-budhi, what life really is. She should start preparing herself for a sorry old age.'

~

Having silenced his brother and his mother, Doso carried on with his Sabar girl. He showed Dulari her place in the house very clearly. She was to do everything that was expected of her—cook, clean, herd cattle—and ask no questions. Dulari submitted meekly to the roles she had been assigned. And within a year of marriage, she bore a son whom they named Saagen.

As Saagen grew up, he became Phuchu's devoted follower. Phuchu, who was called Phuchu-master for his skill at marbles and because of the many other games he knew, taught his younger cousin some of his tricks and techniques. But there was one which he did not teach Saagen, and which became his favourite: Maachis-Kakra, in which Phuchu made a seemingly simple meshwork of matchsticks on the ground. After that he pressed one matchstick to the outer part of the mesh and all the matchsticks would lift magically like the bobbing head of a garden chameleon. This trick was a favourite of nearly all the young boys of Kadamdihi and each time Phuchu visited the village, they would gather around to see Phuchu-master create wonders with matchsticks.

Though Rupi's relationship with her brother-in-law had soured, she could bear no animosity towards Saagen. She bought him clothes and sweets on each visit. And while she knew that Dulari was constantly being compared with her, and knew that Dulari envied her, she hoped that would understand and accept her, if not as a friend then at least as an elder sister-in-law.

Rupi heard Dulari say to Putki one day, 'We don't need their clothes.'

But Putki responded scornfully, 'Be thankful that they are at least buying clothes for your son. What are you doing for Saagen? Do you think you can raise your one son in the way that she has raised three of hers?'

Dulari became hysterical. 'I knew it!' she screamed, 'she has always been your favourite. And why not? She's your elder daughter-in-law, after all. How does it matter that she just keeps lying under the dogor tree all day.'

'Don't shout!' Putki said, adjusting her sari to cover her breasts. 'Can't you see that she is unwell? Had she been healthy like you, she'd have managed the entire house alone. And don't forget, she ran this house alone for more than ten years.'

'Yes,' Dulari said cruelly. 'From Nitra.'

Rupi understood Dulari's predicament. Doso was never around, Putki was always drunk and had to be constantly fetched home, and she was always being compared with the elder daughter-in-law. Rupi decided to reach out to her.

'Mai,' she said to Dulari one day. 'Does Doso still stay away?'

'Are you blind?' Dulari spat.

Dulari's rage ripped Rupi's white flag to shreds. A sharp pain shot through Rupi's aching head.

'I just wanted to know, mai…' Rupi began.

'There is no need to know. Keep to your own family. I will not share my husband or my child with anyone. I know you are too good. Good enough to share your husband and sons with another woman. I can't be as good as you.'

Rupi had made the effort to rise from her bed to go to her sister-in-law so that if she ever shifted to Kadamdihi permanently, she would at least have an ally in the family. After this confrontation, however, she realized that she had no friends at all. She was filled with bitterness for Dulari, and the two sisters-in-law stopped speaking to each other. Dulari built a separate chulha for herself in a corner of the racha. The various lives did not intersect anymore.

As usual, Putki broadcast everything to anyone who was willing to give her a glass of haandi or paura. Word spread through the village and the rift between the respectable Khorda-haram's sons, grandsons of the revered Somai-haram, became the subject of much gossip and speculation.

~

When Dulari finally lost her patience, she began to ask questions.

'Why do you leave me alone?' she asked Doso when he returned home late yet again. 'I can't go running after your mother and manage the house at the same time. You also have a son. Don't forget.'

A vicious slap fell on Dulari's cheek and, before she could react, Doso grabbed her by the hair and flung her out on to the racha. After that, savage kicks and punches fell on her body until she almost passed out.

'Engamem! You have the nerve to ask me questions? You!'

Though Putki was awake when this happened, she did not restrain her son.

After that, the beatings became routine. Doso would come home late and the first thing he would do was to beat his wife. And when he didn't use his hands, he used threat and humiliation.

'I will kick you so hard that you will go flying out of this house. I've done you a favour by marrying you. Be thankful to me and don't ask for anything more,' he would say.

Fed up, Dulari packed her bags one day and left for her father's house, taking Saagen with her. After a fortnight, Doso brought her back. Soon after their return, Doso beat Dulari to within an inch of her life.

A month after the beating, though, things took yet another turn.

Doso did not get out of bed until late afternoon. At around midday, startling news buzzed through Kadamdihi.

'Have you heard? That Kharya girl of Doso's is dead.'

'How? When?'

'This morning. She had fever and diarrhoea. I heard she died begging for a drop of water to drink.'

The Fall of the Strongest Woman
of Kadamdihi

Doso, once an irrepressible bull, became a servile lamb. He no longer visited patas. If he went to a haat, he would just buy whatever Dulari had asked him to and would promptly turn back. He also stopped drinking.

Doso would wake up early each morning and take the cattle and the goats out to graze. He would then sit in one place and leave the animals unsupervised. Whatever happened then, even if the sun shone mercilessly or it rained, he would not move from his spot until noon when he would gather the animals to return home. Several people would pass by him. Many would stop to talk.

'Ched ya, Doso-bhai. Ched khobor?'

'It is too sunny, Doso-bhai. You better move to the shade of that tree.'

He didn't say anything to anyone.

Doso quickly lost weight and hair while Dulari put on weight around her waist and her breasts became heavy. Her malnutritioned, impoverished look vanished. People soon began to talk of how one or the other had seen Dulari on the bank of the Kadamdihi stream on full-moon nights. Her buck teeth, too, began to look less and less ridiculous and more and more fearsome.

The women of the majhi's house sneered. 'Just this remained to be seen. A dahni in Somai-haram's house. What medicine she must have given our Doso!'

~

In Nitra, Rupi could barely get out of bed, even though she religiously took more and more of the herbalist's powders. All she could do was to cook for her family. However, more often than not, she had to depend on Gurubari to cook for all of them.

Gurubari remained sweet and cordial. 'You know, mai,' she said to Rupi one day, 'your hoinhar has finished building our house in Chakuliya. Now he'll try to use his contacts to get transferred to the school in Jirapara and we'll all start living in Chakuliya.'

Rupi only nodded.

Gurubari carried on. 'Purnima is already in college in Tata. We'll send Pansurin to Ranchi, to a hostel. Your hoinhar has friends there. But she must complete school first.'

Rupi thought of her own sons. It had been years since Jaipal had dropped out, even before completing high school. Bishu and Phuchu had both received erratic schooling, what with the constant shuffle between Nitra and Kadamdihi. As it was, they were hardly the studious type. Sido had other things to do, like composing rhymes for pamphlets and drinking with Bairam-master and the majhi; and Rupi's suggestions carried no weight.

Gurubari's daughters were both growing up into beauties. With their looks and their education, they were sure to find good husbands. Even jobs, perhaps. And to compensate for anything else, there was their mother's skills and her gods.

All at once, Rupi did not want to stay in Nitra any more. No. No more.

'Right now, my sister and her husband are staying in our house in Chakuliya,' Gurubari said. 'You need somebody to guard the house and the property, too. Our banana trees there...' Rupi stopped listening. She shut her eyes and tried to sleep so that she wouldn't have to listen to any more of Gurubari's successes.

~

The silver-haired aunt woke Rupi up one night. She followed the fragrance of jasmine out of the room.

Outside, she stopped by her sons' room and heard them snoring. It was a konami night. The racha was a cauldron of milk, bathed in white, and everything was clearly visible. The door of Gurubari's room was ajar. She walked along, hypnotized, unmindful of what lay outside.

She found the outside door open. She stepped out into the kulhi. The jasmine led her to the byre. When Rupi reached the byre, her senses returned.

Four naked women danced to some silent rhythm around what looked like a small animal. Even though the women danced vigorously, and the scene was illuminated by some hidden fire, the cows did not bellow in fright nor did the servant boys rush out of their quarters outside the byre. Rupi turned and fled. She did not bolt the outside door. She rushed into her room, pulled her chador over her head and tried to forget what she had just seen.

Tomorrow, *yes, tomorrow*, she'd tell Sido that she couldn't stay in Nitra any more. She had to return to Kadamdihi with her sons. At any cost.

~

'Are you sure?' Sido asked.

'Yes.'

'Fine, then. Bairam-da is getting himself transferred to either Chakuliya or Jirapara. I'll try to put in my name as well.'

Oh! Rupi thought, nearly hitting her head in exasperation, this Bairam and Gurubari will just not get out of our lives!

~

Jaipal chose to stay back with his father in Nitra while Bishu and Phuchu went along with Rupi. She walked along the platform at the Rakha Mines Railway Station and boarded the train in a daze. Even after Phuchu had found Rupi a seat after the compartment partly emptied at the Ghatshila Railway Station, he had to almost force her on to a seat.

Once she was seated and a spring breeze cooled her face, she fell asleep.

'Yo! Get up.'

'Huh! What?'

'We've reached Chakuliya.'

'We've reached?'

'Yes, now get up. Dada's already walked ahead.' He pointed to Bishu who was making his way through the crowd.

It was spring, the month of Boishakh. The Chakuliya Railway Station was dusty and a mild wind was blowing. There were dark clouds in the sky.

'Looks like rain,' Bishu remarked.

'We won't be able to reach home before it starts,' Phuchu replied.

'We'll have to walk fast.'

While the two brothers talked, Rupi stared blankly at the crowd before her.

Her sons led Rupi out of Chakuliya. The two carried all their bags while Rupi followed. Rupi would usually stop in Chakuliya to buy jobay-laadoo and chop-singhara, treats which Saagen loved, but this was no ordinary visit. She was going to stay in Kadamdihi forever.

The Marwari's tomb had just come into view when they heard a loud crash behind them. They turned to look. Someone's tin roof was being blown about by the wind. It was the Kaalboishakhi, the deadly storm of late spring.

They sprinted, but the clouds were faster. The rain soon began to pelt down with force. Bishu and Phuchu ran into the Marwari's memorial and up on to the platform. Rupi followed close behind. Four travellers were sheltering there from the sudden rain. They made space for Rupi and her sons. While Bishu and Phuchu walked to the centre of the platform, Rupi stood along its edge. The cool spray gave her much needed respite.

'Where are you headed to, babu?' the eldest man in the group asked Phuchu. 'Which village are you from?'

Phuchu answered courteously. 'We are from Kadamdihi. We are going there.'

'I see. Is that lady your mother?'

'Yes, she is our mother. And he is my elder brother.' Phuchu pointed to Bishu who forced a smile.

'How nice! Which house in Kadamdihi are you going to, son?'

'We are going to the house of Khorda-haram.'

'Khorda-haram?' The old man's eyes twinkled. 'Wasn't he Somai-haram's son-in-law? How are you related to Khorda-haram?'

'We are his grandsons.'

'Grandsons! What is your father's name?'

'Sido.'

'Sido!' The man nearly embraced Phuchu out of delight.

'Look here!' he said to his three companions. 'These are Khorda-haram's grandsons, Sido's children. And that,' he pointed to Rupi who looked on silently as the conversation became lively, 'that is Khorda-haram's daughter-in-law. Come here, son,' he called out to Bishu. 'Come closer, baahu,' he called out to Rupi. 'Don't be afraid. You don't know us but we know your family very well. Somai-haram was a very good man. Khorda-haram was also a very good man. There can be no one like them.'

Bishu and Phuchu grinned while Rupi fidgeted in embarrassment. She didn't want to answer any more questions so she decided to remain on the edge of the platform and on the margin of the conversation. The rain had gotten stronger and Rupi was almost drenched.

'How is your father, son?' the old man asked Bishu. 'You don't live here, do you?'

'No, we live in Nitra,' Bishu said. 'That is where our father works. He is fine.'

'I see, I see. So how did you come now? And alone? Where is your father?'

'Uh-uh…' Bishu began and then stopped. Phuchu stared at his brother. The boys had been told that they were going back to Kadamdihi for good, but what reason would they give?

'We…we want to see our grandmother,' Bishu muttered uncertainly.

The old man smiled. 'Ah! That is so nice. It is so nice to see you all, so nice. Come, sit, sit down. Rest awhile. Tell your mother, too.'

'Sure, we will,' Bishu said and turned away. That was the end of the conversation. Rupi heaved a sigh of relief and looked outside the compound through a gap in the wall. The rain was creating pockmarks on the surface of the small stream which flowed alongside. Corpses were cremated along the bank and it was said that witches practised their craft there, feeding on human waste when they could not find a live human to consume.

Rupi was looking out over the compound wall through the misty sheet of rain when she spotted a woman. What could she be doing there in this rain? The woman seemed familiar to Rupi. When the fragrance of jasmine reached Rupi's nostrils, she nearly fell off the platform. She held on to one of the columns and shrieked.

The men rushed over.

'What is it, yo?' Bishu held her by the shoulders. 'What happened?'

She kept screaming.

'Yo, what is it?' Bishu tightened his grip as Rupi wriggled to be let free. 'What happened? What happened?'

'Aaa… aaa… aaa…' Rupi was overwhelmed with fright, so much so that she couldn't speak a proper syllable. She kept staring through the gap in the wall. She clutched at Bishu's shirt so tightly that he could feel her nails dig into his skin. She dragged him towards the other edge of the platform.

The old man was alarmed. 'Mai! Baahu! What's wrong? What happened?'

The other three men were dumbfounded, and so was Phuchu. The entire episode was beyond him.

One of the old man's companions shivered. 'We knew this place was haunted. How long will this rain last?'

They all huddled together.

Rupi lay flat on the ground. Her panic seemed to have ceased. But when Bishu let go of his mother and stood up, she jumped to her feet and ran out of the memorial into the pouring rain.

Bishu dashed off after his mother. Phuchu followed.

They found her under a tamarind tree by the side of the road. She was close to unconsciousness and breathing heavily, though unhurt. They brought her back to the platform, but she had no recollection of what had happened just minutes before. And if she did, she hid it very well. No one said anything and when the rain ebbed some time later, they were the first to leave the Marwari's memorial.

Rupi and her sons did not realize, perhaps, what was to come. While their domestic life was in disarray, a more immediate problem had begun at the Marwari's memorial: the beginning of their complete loss of face in society.

The men would surely narrate this incident to their friends and families. And while there could be many explanations for it, the one which would find the most takers would be that Rupi had seen a ghost. Which would lead to more questions. Why did only she see the ghost? Why didn't she tell them or her sons about it? Why did she run off like a madwoman?

Among Santhals, it is taboo for women to become mediums. Even Jaher-Ayo, the highest female deity of the Sarna pantheon, needs a man to manifest herself. A Santhal woman who behaves in the way Rupi did at the Marwari's memorial can do so only because of two reasons: either a spirit or a dahni had ascended the woman; or, the woman is herself a dahni. And, as most Santhals would never believe that Rupi's body had hosted a spirit or a dahni, only one explanation would remain. Khorda-haram's elder daughter-in-law, too, had become a dahni.

The Next Strongest Woman of Kadamdihi

Dulari became the strongest woman in Kadamdihi. Her strength did not flow from her physical vitality or from her abilities as a home-maker and -manager. Dulari's power came from the knowledge she had received from her cousins in her father's village, the knowledge which made her capable of controlling people by using charms. No one quite had a measure of how powerful Dulari actually was until Singo revealed it all.

~

Singo belonged to the family of the godeth, the village crier. A girl of fourteen, she attended a girls' school in Chakuliya and rode to school on a bicycle which had been given to her by the government of Jharkhand. Because her parents had not been aware of the merits of immunization at the time of her birth, Singo had been afflicted with polio and walked with a limp. Though a lively girl, and one of the prettiest in Kadamdihi, Singo never participated in the usual games children play. When she was a child, she used to see her siblings, cousins and other children of the village run around, climb trees and generally have a great time. She yearned to join them. But they mocked her lameness, calling her Khurdi. Singo would ignore the taunts. She would raise her oversized frocks—hand-me-downs from the more prosperous families of the majhi-gushti—and run in an awkward, uneven gait but at great speed.

When Singo was approaching puberty, her mother sat her down and explained to her that she must now stop running around with the other children. 'Singo, you are now different,' she said. 'You are growing up. Your body is taking a new shape. This is not the age to wear frocks and midis and minis. Or to run around.' So Singo became a demure young girl. She started wearing salwar-jumper and cycled gravely to school everyday. She learnt to walk slowly, trying not to make her limp obvious. Singo was all set to make the perfect entry into womanhood when, one morning, she limped out of her house and started to run.

This wasn't the sprinting of the competitions of her childhood, when she had to run to prove that she was as good as those who were lucky enough not to have contracted polio despite not being immunized. It was definitely not the playful running of adolescence. Singo's mother was a strict lady who kept a close watch on where Singo went and who she spoke to. And with her limp, it was difficult for Singo to venture too far from her mother's keen supervision. Simply stated, there was no reason for Singo to run and, had she reason, there was no way that she could.

When she set off, everybody gaped till her mother came screaming out of the house. 'Singo! Singo! My daughter! Somebody help!'

Singo ran down the length of the Kamar-kulhi and turned towards the house of the majhi. She nearly stopped in front of Putki's house but instead of stopping, she ran around Putki's house, startling Rupi who was lying on the cot under the dogor tree behind the house, and over some fallows till she reached the main kulhi again.

'Where is she? Where is she?' the women chasing Singo asked Putki and Rupi.

'Was that our Singo?' Putki asked.

'Yes.'

'What? How can she run like this?'

'We don't know, jhi. We are all surprised. Where did she go?'

'I don't know. She went somewhere behind our house.'

'There she is!' a man cried. Singo was now running back towards the Kamar-kulhi.

Men, women and children had lined up along the Kamar-kulhi to watch the spectacle. A Kamar man stood in the middle of the kulhi with his arms held out to break her speed. Singo simply knocked the man down and kept running. The men following her tripped over the fallen man and a small stampede ensued. Singo's mother, too, fell down and her father, who was part of the group following Singo, dragged the poor woman into their house and slapped her.

'You wretched woman! It is all your doing. You don't care enough for her. What kind of people is she meeting? And what kind of people are *you* meeting? Who has done this to my daughter?'

Singo's mother broke free and ran to a corner of their racha. 'Don't blame me!' she shouted, 'Don't blame me at all. Right from the time she was a baby, I have never, ever let her out of my sight. Have you done that? You say you care for your children. Have you watched them each moment of their lives? And Singo? How much have you seen her, how much? All day she is with me. Tell me if I am wrong, tell me.'

An elderly aunt from the party following Singo pushed Singo's father away. She said, 'Don't do this now. First you look for your daughter and then decide whose fault it is that your daughter should run around like this.'

'She is headed for the stream,' a boy informed Singo's father and ran off.

When they got there, they found that a circus was under way on the banks of the Kadamdihi stream. The search party was tired. Some men were lying on the ground, keeping watch on the other side of the stream where Singo was jumping over bigna shrubs with a couple of younger men in hot pursuit. Singo's father could see it: the men were tired but his daughter had so much energy, she could still run many kilometres more and jump over many more bigna and khejur shrubs.

An older man nudged Singo's father. 'Son, this does not seem right.'

'What are you saying?' Singo's father, bewildered and tired, asked.

'Call an ojha.'

'You mean… You mean… I was just wondering if it had to do something with…'

'It has everything to do with whatever you were thinking of. Let's go back to the village and summon an ojha.'

'And my daughter?'

'She won't stop. As long as that power is inside her, she won't stop. Let these young men stay here. We'll get them to hem her in from all sides so that she doesn't run out of sight. No one will try to catch her. That will be impossible.'

Singo's father understood. Instructions were communicated hurriedly. The men who had been keeping a watch crossed the stream and shouted instructions to the younger men who were exhausted by now. They, nevertheles, agreed to cooperate.

Singo's father hurried back to the village.

Singo's mother asked, 'Where is my daughter? Why didn't you bring her back?'

He shoved her away.

The same ojha who had performed the soonoom-paanjaa after Khorda-haram's death was summoned. It took more than an hour for him to arrive. Someone ran up from the stream to report that the men there were finding it hard to keep up with Singo. A remedy had to be found quickly.

The ojha placed a jackfruit leaf with some mustard oil on it before him, closed his eyes and mumbled something even as another boy came running from the Kadamdihi stream. He bent over, hands on knees, and panted. Once he'd caught his breath, he said, 'She is coming back.'

The crowd was yet to get over this fresh development when, like a gust of wind, Singo ran into her house and fell to the ground. Her mother rushed to her.

'Singo, get up! Get up!'

Singo did not respond. She stared blankly at the faces around her.

'Who are you?' the ojha asked.

Singo smiled coyly and hid her face in her palms. Some women giggled, others looked terrified. Singo's father went red with anger.

'Who are you?' the ojha asked again.

'No, no,' Singo said from behind cupped palms.

'Tell me, or else you know very well what I can do to you.'

'Dular… Dular…' Singo did not uncover her face, as if she were shy, as if she had done something shameful.

Singo's father was so angry that he grabbed his wife and dragged her to a corner of the room.

'What is she saying?' he shouted. 'Dular dular. Why is she saying dular? Does she know a boy? Is she having an affair?'

His anger was justified. Dular means love or lover.

'Is this really about a boy?' people in the crowd whispered.

'Does she want to get married?' someone asked.

'How many times I told her mother that Singo was growing up, and to look for a husband for her. But no one will look at her because of her limp,' another woman said.

Singo's father slapped his wife's face again.

'I have done nothing,' the woman shouted. 'Don't hit me, it's not my fault.'

Some men held Singo's father back. In the melee, Singo slinked away.

'Catch her, somebody,' the people shouted.

'No, wait,' the ojha said. 'Let her go. We'll follow her.'

Singo walked in a trance through the entire Kamar-kulhi. Rows of men, women and children tracked each of her steps while a group followed closely. There were people on both sides of the kulhi. Surprisingly, however, the space outside Putki's house was vacant. Not only this, even their front door was shut. This was unusual, for doors were kept open during the daytime. It was as if Putki's family expected trouble.

Singo plopped before Putki's door.

'Dulari… Dulari… I am Dulari,' she said and fainted.

It was clear to everyone. Singo was quite innocent. It was Dulari who had thrown away her good sense and had cast one of her spells upon the innocent young girl.

Who can tell why a dahni does what she does? It could be that something about Singo had attracted Dulari: perhaps her youth, her vivacity, or her bright smile. It could be that these were the very qualities in Singo which Dulari resented. It could even be that Dulari was simply testing the effect and the extent of her powers. The reason could have been anything, but the consequences were the same: a young girl was publicly humiliated and a middle-aged dahni stood exposed.

'How shameless Doso's wife has become!' Singo's father exclaimed.

Hansda Sowvendra Shekhar

Others were non-committal. 'Is there any use talking to him about it?' they asked each other.

'I tell you, we should drag her out of her house and give her a beating,' Singo's father raged. 'She destroyed her husband and she devoured her husband's lover, isn't her stomach full now? How many more lives does she intend to end? Our children are not safe in our own village.'

'Relax, relax,' said the man who had advised Singo's father to return home and engage the ojha. 'We cannot do anything to Dulari now. Yes, she has become a nuisance. But who are you going to talk about it to? Doso is not in his senses any more. Sido is now under the influence of Bairam's wife, we all know that. His wife has been taken over, too. Their children, all of them, are under the power of either Bairam's wife or Dulari. Putki has grown old. She won't live for long, we can all see that. That family will face its own punishment. No one needs to say or do anything. Just keep a check on your children. Make sure that we don't mix too freely with their family.'

This was easier said than done. Kadamdihi wasn't the village it once was. The men of yore had believed in keeping the village safe by placing it in the hands of the good gods. Somai-haram, for one, had been very particular about organizing worships at the jaher. But now, the people of Kadamdihi had stopped worshipping their gods. The Baha and Maak-Moray festivals were not being organized any more. The jaher had turned into a jungle. Furthermore, the Santhals of Kadamdihi had started depending on frauds to protect their village and their faith, as was evident from the number of people who had become members of a cult called the Marang-Buru Sabha.

This Marang-Buru Sabha was founded by a baba who used to work as a cleaner of trucks in Baharagora. After changing several jobs—he was a mechanic, then a miner, and then a labourer—he claimed to have received a divine message and became a godman. His fame spread and his cult grew. His followers included people from many communities, all of them Hindus, who spent generously at his gatherings.

Lately though, Santhals too had been attracted by the baba's charm and had started attending his gatherings. It was said that the baba had started the Marang-Buru Sabha keeping in mind his Santhal followers. The Marang-Buru Sabha advertised heavily. Many houses in Kadamdihi had the image of a trishul and the name, Marang-Buru Sabha, etched on their walls in blue and red. The Marang-Buru Sabha usually met in Dhalbhumgarh, where the followers gathered to chant Marang-Buru! Marang-Buru! Marang-Buru!—as if Marang-Buru was a Hindu deity who could be propitiated with chants. What was even more astonishing was that people who didn't have enough money for their families, too, donated money to the baba's fund.

There was another interesting thing regarding the Santhals who were followers of the Marang-Buru Sabha. The Santhals from Kadamdihi who went to Dhalbhumgarh regularly to chant Marang-Buru! Marang-Buru! at the Sabha's gatherings all came from families in which at least one woman was known to be a dahni. It wasn't clear what drew them to the baba. It could have been the baba's charisma. Or it could be that after having worshipped the bad gods, they wanted to curry favour with the highest deity of the Sarna pantheon.

Furthermore, what only a few women knew earlier, many had now learnt. It was being said that in Kadamdihi, the Kamar dahni attacked their victims with freshly forged scythes while the Kunkal dahni skinned their victims with the sharp shards of broken clay tiles. All of them were being led by Dulari. Kadamdihi was no longer safe.

The Clash of the Equals

Sido returned to Kadamdihi and Bairam to Chakuliya for good.
Both of them had received transfers to the primary school in
Jirapara. They would travel to and from school from their
respective villages. Purnima and Pansurin were both in Ranchi;
they studied at the university there and stayed in a girls' hostel
in the Tharpakhna area. Jaipal used Gurubari and Bairam's
house in Chakuliya as a base for his visits to different patas.
Mostly, he would drink, brawl and, too drunk to return home
to Kadamdihi, spend the night in Gurubari's house and go back
to Kadamdihi the morning after.

Bishu had taken over the farming along with his uncle Doso.
Doso was a man lost, uncertain of his steps, unaware of the
paths he trod. He often mumbled to himself as he walked
through the village, clothed only in two gumchhas, one tied
around his waist and another thrown across his shoulders. Spit
dribbled down the corners of his mouth when he spoke. He had
become more and more like an automaton, becoming fit for
work only when Dulari ordered him to perform one task or the
other.

Bishu was unlike his elder brother, Jaipal. A silent, thoughtful
young man, he spent most of his time in fields, sitting in the
shade of a tree or on an aaday, a twig of khor between his lips,
staring at the wide expanse of earth before him. In the absence

of his father and elder brother, and with his uncle infirm, it was Bishu who did the shopping for the family. The necessities: oil and salt, sugar, spices, wheat flour—the last for Sido, who had been diagnosed with diabetes and couldn't eat rice. Bishu bought medicines for his mother, checked her temperature, sat with her under the dogor tree and talked with her about their family— his father, especially.

'Has your father returned?'

'No, he hasn't.'

'He did not eat again. I rolled the rutis for him.'

'You don't worry. He will certainly eat somewhere.'

'Where? Where is he going to eat? At that Gurubari's?'

Bishu said nothing.

She would ask about Jaipal, her eldest, her favourite. The one she couldn't call her own any more. 'Has your dada returned?'

'No.'

'Tell me, how many days has it been?'

'It's been just one day.'

'One day? Where does he think he's going to eat and sleep? Who is going to feed him?'

'He must be at Gurubari-marak-ayo's…'

'Don't! Don't. She's not your marak-ayo.'

Phuchu, the master of tricks, the puzzle-solver, did not devise any more tricks and puzzles. He forgot the games of his childhood as he shuffled towards adulthood in silence, his corpulent frame swaying from side to side.

The people of Kadamdihi spoke about all this in hushed tones.

'Do you see them? Sido's children. How they've changed!'

'That Phuchu, we used to call him Phuchu-mastar, didn't we? He was so clever. What has happened to him? He looks like an imbecile.'

'It's the effect of that Gurubari's magic.'
'Certainly, there's no doubt about that.'

~

Bairam died on one konami night. It was a simple death; he did not suffer. Of course, it could never be proven, but everyone said that his death was just one more instance of Gurubari's skill. While several theories about his death were discussed, everyone generally accepted that Bairam had been sacrificed.

Bairam's death may or may not have been a sacrifice, but it did benefit Gurubari in one way. He had died two years before he was due to retire. This entitled one member of his family to a government job on compassionate grounds. Gurubari was made an office attendant in the teachers' training school Bairam and Sido once attended. Her literacy helped.

After Bairam's death, Sido spent practically every day in Gurubari's house in Chakuliya, returning home to Kadamdihi only at night.

~

One morning, Dulari was at the well near the dogor tree. Rupi, who had just been woken up by yet another dream of the white-haired aunt, squinted in the bright sunlight and began mumbling. 'Shameless woman! Look at what you have become. A witch! A dirty woman!'

Dulari could not understand the reason for this sudden attack. It was true, the relationship between the sisters-in-law had gone from bad to worse over the years, but both of them took care to stay out of each other's way. Dulari hardly ever spoke directly to Rupi. If she had to vent her anger, she did so to Putki. And if she had to address Rupi, she only said 'your elder daughter-in-law' or 'that queen under the dogor tree'.

They had had no fights lately, the two sisters-in-law. And that day, Dulari was following her usual routine. After carrying water from the well to the kitchen, she would have drawn Rupi's bath. Perhaps it was Rupi's helplessness at having to depend on the woman she hated so much which gave rise to her sudden outburst.

'You think no one knows what you're up to, you dirty woman?'

Dulari stopped, put the bucket down, and stood still.

'You'll eat us all, that is what you intend to do, no? Tell me, you shameless woman. Why are you standing still? What are you waiting for?'

Dulari walked up to Rupi's cot.

'You think you are very good, dai?' she asked Rupi. 'Tell me, what good has your goodness done to you?'

Rupi was shaken out of her sudden and mistimed anger. She wasn't shouting at Dulari because she wanted to pick a fight. She was just tired of lying about like a corpse, she was tired of being dependent on others, she was tired of not having her husband and firstborn with her, she was tired of knowing what ailed her but not its cure. She was tired of her disease. Her anger wasn't directed at Dulari; it was her anger against all women who performed magic.

Dulari, however, was in no mood to study Rupi's psyche. 'Tell me, dai, what good has your goodness done to you?' she asked again.

Rupi's head ached at this turning of the tables.

'You accuse me of being a witch. You say that I'm going to devour you all. Yes, I am a witch but let me tell you, it's not me who's eating you up.'

Rupi just stared.

'You know very well who is feeding off you,' Dulari said. 'But tell me, dai, if you are so good, what is your goodness doing? Why isn't it saving you from being devoured? I may be a witch, but tell me, did I have a way out? What was mine was being taken away from me. I had to claim it for myself. What other way did I have? Who would've helped me? No one. No one, dai. I had to help myself. I had to do everything by myself. If it meant using dahni-bidya, I was ready for that. I had to reclaim what was rightfully mine. Tell me, dai, did I do anything wrong? I don't think so. If you are so good, use your goodness to get back what you have lost.'

Alternative Therapies

After allopathy and naturopathy had failed, Sido, at the insistence of well-wishers, turned to homoeopathy. The practitioner he took Rupi to was a Mahato man. His clinic was in a rented room on the ground floor of a two-storeyed house in the Nutan Bazaar area of Chakuliya, on the other side of the railway crossing.

It was a swelteringly hot summer day. Rupi looked suitably sick as they waited in front of the doctor's chambers. The waiting area was deserted; very few people seemed to be using the doctor's services. Perhaps it was the weather that kept patients away. It was a day to remain indoors, in the cool comfort of mud houses.

Squinting in the bright sunlight, her head low, Rupi did not look around her. She was disinterested in a cure. She was tired, and the bougainvillea vine which climbed up the side of the veranda to the floor above provided meagre shade. She shut her eyes and grimly endured the throbbing behind her forehead.

~

Sido had been extremely gung-ho about the homoeopathy doctor.

'I think I have found a cure for you,' he had said to Rupi one evening. He must have really been excited, for that day he had returned home very early, even before sunset.

'There is a homyopathy daktar in Chakuliya,' he had said excitedly. 'He must surely have something for you. I wonder how I did not know of him all this time.'

Rupi often wondered how he came upon these fantastic ideas of his when everything was so clearly evident. Yet there was nothing she could do about her husband's desire to cure her. So she had woken up early on the day of the appointment, bathed, eaten breakfast, and prepared to leave. Sido had called an autorickshaw to take them to Chakuliya. The vehicle, too, came at the right time. It was Sido who delayed. In his excitement at having found a possible cure for his wife, he had taken time to get ready. When they had finally climbed into the autorickshaw, they had been nearly an hour behind schedule. Add to the stress of the day the agony of travelling over the bumpy road between Kadamdihi and Chakuliya, and Rupi had been fatigued and queasy even before she stepped out of the autorickshaw.

The homoeopath's clinic, it had seemed to her, presented an exaggerated sense of his qualifications and abilities. A huge signboard hung above the veranda.

Dr M. Mahato
B.H.M.S.

the signboard read in the Roman and Bangla scripts. Roman on top, Bangla at the bottom. And wherever one looked, there were red crosses. There was one on each side of the name of the doctor. Just above the front door which opened into the homoeopath's chamber was a smaller board which had the same text printed in Roman and Devanagari. Red crosses had been painted on the frame above the door like the auspicious swastika; there were crosses on the pillars which supported the upper storey. The homoeopath's motorcycle parked outside had red crosses painted on both the back and the front licence plates. It was difficult to miss that Dr Mahato was, indeed, a man of medicine.

It seemed to Rupi that the homoeopath was taking an intolerably long time with each patient. When she and Sido had arrived, one patient was in his chamber and two were waiting outside. Rupi had thought they'd be done soon and return to Kadamdihi in the same autorickshaw that they had come in. But time passed and even the tiny queue that they were part of did not inch forward at all. In the meantime, the autorickshaw driver asked to be let off. Sido agreed, but reluctantly.

When they finally sat facing the homoeopath, Rupi could understand why it had taken them so long. The man asked many, many questions about everything; from her diet to her family. To Rupi, the meeting was a blur, like all her other appointments with other medicine-men. Sido answered all the questions the homoeopath asked Rupi. The doctor took her pulse and, like a doctor of allopathy, checked her chest with a stethoscope. It took him a long time to ask all his questions and make his examinations. Rupi realized that the homoeopath was a very patient man. Not only was he patient, he was very soft-spoken, too. Luckily, she had Sido sitting by her side. And the homoeopath didn't seem to mind. Unlike other doctors he did not insist that Rupi answer his questions herself.

By the time she was handed a small phial filled with tiny white pellets—whose confusing dosages were explained to Sido—Rupi was dying to lie down somewhere.

~

'Just a little further,' Sido said as he led Rupi along the railway tracks. She followed in a daze.

They reached the station building and emerged from the station compound. Sido took her to a row of houses on the outskirts of Chakuliya.

'There it is.' He pointed to a house with a number of banana trees in the courtyard. 'Just a little more.'

Rupi couldn't understand where her husband was leading her to. Or why he should smile when he pointed to the house.

She understood just minutes later.

Standing at the door of that house, welcoming them, was a beaming Gurubari.

Has she really been widowed? was Rupi's first thought. On Gurubari's face was the contentment of a woman who has achieved everything she set out to. Though she was dressed in white—an expensive-looking, crisply ironed cotton sari with needlework flowers along the border—and did not wear sindoor in the parting of her hair, she still wore gold earrings and bangles.

'Rupi-mai,' she cooed, 'it has been so long. I am so happy to see you. Jaipal's father was saying that you are not keeping well again nowadays. What's the matter?'

Jaipal's father? Rupi had never heard Gurubari address Sido so intimately. He was always Sido, or babu—like a younger brother or a younger brother-in-law. 'Jaipal's father' seemed so strange. But she said nothing.

'You must be tired,' Gurubari said. 'It's so hot outside. Wait, I'll get you something cold to drink.'

Rupi looked around her, opening her eyes wide to dispel fatigue. So this was the house Bairam-master had built for his wife.

'See, this is the house your hoinhar built for me and my daughters,' Gurubari said from the kitchen. 'But who lives here? No one. Both Purnima and Pansurin are in Ranchi. They come home only on holidays. So I've got my younger sister and her children to stay with me.'

'Yes,' Rupi mumbled, looking at Gurubari's two teenaged nieces.

'It was really very nice of Jaipal's father to help us settle down,' Gurubari said. 'He helped my daughters, too, when they were settling down in their hostel in Ranchi. He goes to see them there. He's such a big help, just like a father figure to my two girls.'

Oh! So that explained why he was always absent. Gurubari did not read her mind now. Though she did reveal something else.

'All of us women in this house.' Gurubari brought out two glasses of cool orange squash on a tray. 'Jaipal sleeps some nights with us and that makes us feel safe.'

'Yes,' Rupi mumbled again.

'He stayed up late last night. He's still sleeping.'

'Jaipal's here?' Rupi nearly choked on the cloyingly sweet drink.

'Yes.' Gurubari pointed to a distant room. 'In that room.'

Sido was laughing as he sipped his drink. 'He is like that,' he said, 'he has always been so. Sleeping in the morning.'

So this is what he likes nowadays: sweet, coloured water.

'Isn't the drink sweet?' Gurubari asked. 'Jaipal's father bought it that day. I was too busy to go shopping. You know, I'm working at the teachers' training school.'

Though stunned by the news, Rupi was careful to not let any thought enter her mind.

'You must eat with us,' Gurubari offered.

'Yes,' Rupi mumbled, ate the lunch Gurubari served them, and slept till late after sunset. Later, she returned with Sido to Kadamdihi in an autorickshaw Jaipal summoned for them. She did not ask her son if he'd come home or stay at Gurubari's.

~

The homoeopathy pellets did not work. They visited the homoeopath two more times and, on both occasions, it became clear that Sido's enthusiasm for the remedy had vanished.

The homoeopath advised patience. 'Homoeopathy attacks the root of the ailment,' he said.

'But the patient is not feeling better at all,' Sido protested.

'I'm better,' Rupi said. 'I'm better. Let's go.'

She couldn't bear to be in that dusty clinic, listening to theories about drugs and diseases she could not understand. Being ill at home is far more preferable to being healthy in a clinic like this, she thought. And she did not want to go to Gurubari's house again. She knew, the more they delayed at the homoeopath's, the greater was their chance of going to Gurubari's house for cool drinks and lunch.

Jaipal bothered her. She could let him spend his days and nights in Gurubari's house. She could see him return home drunk, unaware where he was stepping next. What she couldn't bear was his bringing home a woman she had no idea about. At least that was what Putki told her he would do. Putki had become very old. She was well over seventy, perhaps eighty years old. She was frailer than ever, she walked with a stoop and had long stopped caring if one breast dangled out of her sari or both. Her drinking continued, though. And what she reported to Rupi was what everyone had been saying about Jaipal.

'From some village outside Chakuliya, they say. I'm not sure,' Putki lisped. 'They say Gurubari must know about that girl.'

'Why Gurubari? Who is Gurubari? Why should she know and not I?'

Putki couldn't look at her daughter-in-law's face, marked with shock and sorrow. Putki avoided moments like this. Her throat felt parched, she needed a drink; a baati of haandi, a glass of paura, anything. As she turned around to leave, she heard Rupi sob. The sob carried sadness that was too heavy to be borne. She willed herself to not listen and walked off towards the majhi's house.

~

On the advice of some well-wishers, Sido decided to try yet another cure. This, he was told, should've been tried some fifteen to twenty years earlier, when Rupi had just begun to display the first symptoms of her condition. When told about this line of treatment, Sido wasn't entirely in favour of it. It was something he had been avoiding—or was being made to avoid—for a long time. Someone suggested an ojha who lived near Chakuliya, in the same village where Doso's lover once lived. The ojha's house was set apart from the other houses.

'She looks entirely fine to me,' the ojha said. 'I don't think that she has any disease.'

'But she has been suffering so much all these years,' Sido said distractedly, aching to get away from it all.

'I can see the suffering she's been going through.' The ojha read Rupi's pale face intently, as if it were a handbook on human diseases printed in an indecipherable script. 'That's why I say,' here he paused for effect, 'her sufferings are not due to some disease. They're coming from…from…'

'What?' Sido, unable to stand the suspense, prompted.

'…the outside,' the ojha said, his answer as perplexing as his diagnosis. 'From the outside.'

'What does that mean?' Sido asked. Rupi looked away. The session was proving to be tiresome.

'Son, do you know how your father died?' the ojha asked calmly, bringing his face close to Sido's, speaking loud enough for only Sido to hear. He did not want to give Rupi any more shocks.

'No,' Sido said, fumbling for a moment for the right words. 'I wasn't there. How does it matter?'

'It matters,' the ojha said. 'There's a similarity between your father's death and your wife's ailment.'

Sido became serious. Where was this headed? he wondered.

'Do you know or not?'

Sido shook his head.

'Listen.' The ojha bent closer towards Sido. 'There were two women. Bad, bad women. They took your father away.'

Sido's head reeled.

'Do you know any bad woman?'

'No, no.' Sido fumbled.

The ojha was surprised. He peered into Sido's face and intently studied each line, each contour, each pore. He looked into Sido's eyes, Sido looked away. The ojha was puzzled. How could this man deny knowing a bad woman when he shared more than just an acquaintance with one?

Then he understood. Perhaps it wasn't a good idea to broach this topic in front of his wife. He looked at Rupi. She looked lost; her eyes were like stones. It isn't a mystery, the ojha thought. I can help you, poor woman. I can see who is doing this to you. But the truth must come first, and your treatment lies entirely in the hands of your man.

'Er... You mind coming inside?' The ojha pointed to a dark room behind him.

Sido hesitated. He looked at the dark room, straining to see inside. He caught a glimpse of fine wisps of smoke which emanated from the upper part of the door. Whatever happened, he wasn't entering an ojha's sanctum sanctorum.

The ojha sensed Sido's reluctance and laughed. He thought, Here is a man who has been completely taken over by a woman who is out to ruin his home, and he suspects me. He lowered his head so that his clients would not be offended by his laughter.

Sido wasn't. He was in no position to feel offended. Rupi was indifferent.

'Come in, please.' The ojha directed his stern, unflinching gaze at Sido's eyes. 'This is important. Do you want your wife to be cured or not? Or are you happy with running from one doctor to another, and with all of them telling you that your wife is absolutely healthy?'

Sido turned towards Rupi and said, 'Stay here, I'll be right back.' He then got up and followed the ojha into his sanctum.

Dhuna smouldering in a dondo gave off dense smoke which dried out Sido's throat. Sido swallowed saliva and tried to accustom himself to the darkness in the room. When his eyes had adjusted, he could see that the dondo and the other objects of worship had been placed before a tall statue of the goddess Kali which stood against the wall. The statue, which rose from the floor to the rafters above, seemed like a near-exact representation of how Kali would have looked had she been real. The figure of Kali was black. Black like coal, black like the night, black like the darkness which engulfed the room. The wisps of dhuna smoke which rose from the dondo floated like rudderless clouds on a dark, moonless night. There was a garland of human heads around the deity's neck. The heads, somehow, seemed real to Sido. He shivered. He looked past the goddess' garlanded torso and froze. The goddess had huge eyes and a protruding tongue so red that it looked like it had been smeared with real blood. Just as his knees were about to give way, the ojha grabbed Sido by his shoulders and sat him on a gaando.

'You shall not lie,' the ojha instructed sternly. 'You are sitting before the goddess. You will not lie at all.'

Sido was uneasy. He couldn't breathe. The smoke from the dhuna made his throat itch. He inhaled hard through his nostrils. He wanted to escape.

'There is a woman,' the ojha said. 'Don't tell me there isn't.'

'Yes, there is.' The acceptance was involuntary. Sido was surprised. What had he said? His forehead beaded with sweat.

'She was once married.'

'Yes, yes.'

Sido wanted to run.

'She is destroying your family, don't you realize that? Your eldest son already belongs to her. Can't you see…'

We must leave! someone screamed into Sido's ears.

Sido stood up straight, his hands by his side, his eyes gazing up at the rafters. A deep, gurgling sound came from his throat.

'What are you doing here?' the ojha screamed at the woman who had suddenly appeared behind Sido. 'Where did you come from?'

The naked apparition held Sido by the arms and screamed into his ears, 'Come with me!' He fell limp. The woman steadied him. She then looked into the ojha's face and snarled, 'I'm taking him away! I dare you to stop me. I pray to the goddess, and I have other gods too. And don't forget, I have made better sacrifices than you. Don't try to scare him. Don't tell him that he is sitting before the goddess. She is my goddess, not yours.'

The ojha stared unbelievingly into Gurubari's face. Her naked body was muscular and lithe like a panther's, and displayed no signs of ageing. She dragged Sido outside.

Sido stumbled out. Rupi rushed to him. 'Why did you push him out?' she shouted at the ojha. 'Are you going to cure me or kill my husband?'

The enemy was too powerful, the ojha understood. She had invaded his house, his very sanctum, to whisk her victim away. She had become too powerful to be stopped by ordinary montros. She couldn't be stopped. No, no, I can't handle her, he thought. I can't handle someone who has devoured people. I don't care. I must save myself first.

'I can't cure you,' the ojha shouted from inside the room.

'Then why did you…' Rupi began when Sido held her back.

'Stop, stop, let's go,' he said

'Why did he take you in there, then?'

'For nothing,' Sido said, leading her away from the ojha's house. 'He was showing me the place where he made sacrifices and kept asking strange questions. When I realized he was useless, I left.'

Good riddance, Sido thought as he pushed his bicycle and Rupi walked behind him, I'll never come back to this place.

'Is This How You Talk to Your Mother?'

Jaipal brought Dumni home on Sido's new motorcycle. Sido had already fallen off it twice.

'Sido-mastar, is this the age to ride motorcycles?' the men in the village had jeered when he had first fallen down trying to learn how to ride it.

'A man is never too old to learn anything,' Sido had answered with a smile.

'Very good,' the men had whispered among themselves. 'And one is never too old to ride a colleague's widow, too.'

However, they had shouted out a cheery reply, 'You are right, Sido-mastar. You are our inspiration.'

After failing to master the machine, Sido went back to his bicycle and handed the motorcycle over to his sons, who took turns to ride it. It was Jaipal's turn when he used it to bring Dumni to Gurubari's house, where they stayed for about a week, and then he brought his bride home.

Dumni was the daughter of a sharecropper from a village which was so insignificant that Rupi didn't even know its name. Dumni sold haandi with her sisters at one of the patas which Jaipal visited with his friends. A few drinks down, both had fallen in love and, two months later, Dumni packed her good clothes in a ragged satchel, sat pillion on Jaipal's motorcycle and fled home. Bishu and Phuchu knew of their brother's affair, but they had decided to keep it from their mother. The silence with which her family had shrouded Jaipal's romance hurt Rupi further.

Jaipal's wedding was put together by Dulari. She kept stealing proud glances at Rupi through the entire proceedings as it was she, the groom's aunt, who was managing the wedding. Once the marriage was satisfactorily conducted, Dulari would be one up on Rupi and she was proud of it.

The wedding was a simple affair, a mere formality to make Dumni part of Sido's family. It lasted just one evening and Rupi squinted through it, for keeping her eyes open for too long gave her a headache. That was the excuse she gave to the women who had gathered, and they all gossiped about the reasons for Rupi's headache. Dumni was one, certainly. And Dulari who, with her conceited airs, was standing in for Rupi as the mistress of the house. There was also the secrecy which had surrounded Jaipal's affair, and Gurubari's involvement, too.

'Who wouldn't have headaches?' the women asked one another.

There had been no time to dye new dhotis for the marriage. A few old unused ones had been hastily taken out of storage trunks and sunned. New clothes had been bought only for Jaipal and Dumni. Someone from the majhi-gushti lifted Jaipal on to his shoulder; Doso lifted Dumni in the dowrah and a half-hearted 'Hori bol Hori' was chanted when Jaipal, looking very pleased with himself, piled sindoor in the parting of Dumni's hair.

Two goats from Sido's byre were slaughtered for the feast. No one from Dumni's family was invited to the wedding, or even informed about it, for it was assumed that she had left her home for good. Also, she had spent more than a fortnight in Jaipal's house without being married to him. The formalities of the gonong and the meeting of village elders were taken care of later.

It was only after the marriage had taken place that everybody realized how small the house was. Putki was an only child, yet the far-sighted Somai-haram had built enough rooms in his house so that both of Putki's sons could be accommodated. However, they weren't enough. Putki's grandchildren needed more rooms.

'I don't have any place to keep my clothes,' Dumni complained one morning.

'Why, baahu?' Rupi asked. 'Jaipal has a box of his own. Use it.'

Dumni went away in a huff. That afternoon, the rice that she cooked was an inedible paste.

Rupi said, 'Why did you take it off the chulha at all? You should have cooked it till it turned completely into water. You don't know how to cook rice and yet you want a separate place to keep your clothes? How many clothes has your rich father given you? You just sat behind my son on the motorcycle and eloped. Did anyone from your family even enquire about your whereabouts?'

Whatever link had still survived between mother and son snapped after this altercation. Dumni stayed home all day, doing nothing, and Jaipal spent all his time in Gurubari's house.

'What are you doing, son? You have a wife now, have you thought about your future and what you are going to do?' Rupi, unable to hold herself any more, finally asked one day.

'That is not your business. You are not feeding us.' Jaipal did not even look at his mother as he said this. It took Rupi all her strength to suppress the pain that had started building up just behind her forehead. She grabbed Jaipal's shoulder and turned him around to face her.

'Is this how you talk to your mother?' she shouted. 'Is this why I gave birth to you, fed you, grew you up? Tell me. You bring home a woman and forget who is who. What, son?' She began panting. She leaned against the wall behind her and squatted. The pain inside her skull was unbearable, but not as much as her son's conduct. Dulari watched them from one end of the racha, Putki from the other. Dulari smiled to herself.

'You have grown me up?' Jaipal shook with anger. 'You have no shame, lying maiju? *You* have grown me up? Say this one more time and see what I do to you. Gurubari-marak-ayo has grown me up. She fed and clothed me. You couldn't even keep your eyes open or your hands from shaking. If I hear one more word from you about me or my wife, remember, that will be the end of you.'

Jaipal had come so threateningly close to Rupi that Dulari stopped smiling and Putki did not walk out of the house as she had intended. They just stepped on to the racha, ready to pounce on Jaipal if he lost his composure. He didn't. Instead, he stalked right out of the house. Dulari and Putki rushed to Rupi and held her in their arms. Rupi was breathless by this time, sobbing, hiccuping and shivering. Her eyes had rolled back into her skull.

'What's wrong, baahu?' Putki hollered. 'Baahu! Baahu!'

'Dai! Dai!' Dulari shouted. 'Talk to us!'

The sobs stopped and a low rattling sound came from Rupi's throat.

They lifted her up and put her on a parkom.

'What to do, Doso-baahu?' Putki asked.

'I don't know, yo.' Dulari said. 'The men are never home when one needs them and whenever they are, this is what they do to us. You stay with dai, I'll go and see. Saagen should be around somewhere, or Bishu.'

Dulari glared at Dumni, who had been watching the entire episode from behind the door of the room she shared with Putki, and rushed out into the kulhi, shouting, 'Saagen! Saagen!' Her message was passed on by one person after the other until it reached Bishu, who was sitting at a grocer's on the road outside Kadamdihi, and Saagen, who was playing football by the stream. They both ran home.

'Does she need medicines? A doctor?' Bishu asked Dulari.

'I don't know, son,' Dulari said. 'You just see her once.'

'Yo! Yo!' Bishu wiped Rupi's face with cold water. She opened her eyes, saw everyone, and broke into tears.

'Whichever woman endangers my mother's life like this has no right to live in this house,' Bishu declared, throwing a sideways glance at Dumni. 'Let her know this, let her husband know this. If something happens to my mother, I will kill them both.'

Late in the evening, Jaipal and Dumni left without telling anyone. Two days later, word reached that they were staying with Dumni's family.

~

A bride for Bishu was suggested by those generous members of the majhi-gushti who couldn't bear to see Sido's two other sons bring home wives who would first complain that the house was too small and take their husbands away with them to their fathers' houses, only to return when faced with the harsh realities of life. Jaipal returned as impulsively as he had left, wife in tow. There had been quarrels in Dumni's home nearly every day the entire month Jaipal was there, Putki reported to Rupi. No one said this directly to Putki or to anyone in her family, but she got this information anyway.

'A guti's house, what will they know?' she lisped.

'This is what happens when servants' daughters are married to kings' sons,' Rupi said.

'They are saying that Jaipal's father-in-law told him to earn his keep instead of freeloading at his wife's house.' Putki's eyes were lowered, Rupi couldn't read them.

Her helplessness ignited anger in Rupi once more. She was furious with her firstborn, but she was also angry with her mother-in-law. This woman, who couldn't live an hour without haandi, who bartered the family's secrets for a moment's intoxication. This woman, who had once freely given herself away in rice mills and at patas. This woman who had once changed men with the seasons. This, her mother-in-law. Rupi was filled with disgust for her.

'They don't even know how to speak to a son-in-law,' Rupi said. She could barely hear her own voice. She spoke for the sake of speaking, for there was something in her mind that needed to be said out loud. 'In our Kadamdihi, sons-in-law are worshipped like gods, for in them lies the good of our daughters. They forget that our Jaipal has done them a favour by marrying their daughter, by bringing her out of the manure-pit that their village is. Who would have been so kind to pick this whore of a girl and bring her to a place like Kadamdihi? She would have eloped with anyone, any servant-boy, any cowherd-boy, any man working in those rice mills and quarries. She was lucky our Jaipal chose her or she would have spent her entire life selling haandi at patas and swinging from one man to the next.'

Rupi looked at Putki. She wasn't sure if Putki had heard her, for her head was lowered. But this was something she wanted Putki to hear. She wanted Putki to know how much she had begun to hate her and others of her kind, like that Dumni.

Yet all her anger was useless now, it wouldn't change anything. Jaipal had come back home. He wasn't wiser, but he was quieter than before. As was Dumni, who cooperated with the new sleeping arrangements that were made. Jaipal and she moved into Putki's room while Putki shifted into Rupi's. The rest of the men—Sido, Doso and their sons—moved to a separate room. Dulari slept alone. For Bishu and his bride-to-be, separate arrangements would have to be made.

However, Bishu was not demanding at all. He knew how to adapt. And if the people of the gushti who were involved in making the match were to be believed, Bishu's bride would be the next Rupi of Kadamdihi. For she was healthy and strong, and as fair as Rupi had been when she got married to Sido.

~

Rupali was from a village near Jhargram in West Bengal. Sido and Doso made the journey to see the bride with four other men of the gushti. They took the ten o'clock passenger train and reached in time for lunch. Simple people they were, the girl's family, yet they served Ingreji paura to their guests, with desi chicken. The girl's father was a farmer and besides the daughter in question, he had four more children: two daughters and two sons.

There were no ostentatious displays of family status; the days of Somai-haram and Khorda-haram were long gone. Somai-haram's family had lost the sheen which once made fathers grow excited at the prospect of giving their daughters in marriage to Putki and Khorda's sons. Putki and Khorda's sons were not perfect; their flaws had caused their family to suffer. This was one of the reasons why the well-wishers of Putki's family had arranged for a match so far away from Kadamdihi. They did not want even a whiff of the scandals surrounding the family to reach the family of any prospective bride.

Rupi's absence was excused with the explanation that she was not keeping well. The bride had to be responsible too, so that she could look after her mother-in-law.

The girl's parents were more than willing to make Sido happy. 'Don't worry, don't worry,' they said. 'Our daughter has been taught everything; you need not worry at all.'

They knew about Somai-haram. 'Who doesn't?' they asked. 'Santhals near and far know about him.'

Thankfully, they were not up to date with recent developments.

'We are so lucky you came to us to see our daughter,' the girl's father said. 'Our daughter will be the happiest woman on earth.'

Sido was hesitant to accept such a claim. He hadn't been so reserved even when he had gone to see Rupi all those years ago.

'What is your name?' he asked softly.

'Tell him, mai,' the girl's mother prompted.

'Rupali,' the girl raised her eyes slightly and said.

'What?' Sido asked.

'Again, mai,' the mother prompted.

This time the girl was louder. 'Rupali,' she said.

The Cure? Well, Almost

Sido was to retire in a few months and Jaipal's wife was seven months pregnant when Bishu's wedding took place. It was a plain, low-key affair. Rupali's father was given five rupees and a pair of goats as the bride price, as well as a pant-piece and a shirt-piece. The goats were procured locally, from a haat near Jhargram. When Rupali's father bid farewell to his daughter, he loaded her and Bishu with gifts. There were saris and ornaments for the daughter, clothes for the son-in-law, a mobile phone, a colour TV with a DTH connection for their household. 'That jhingalala they say, jawai,' one of Bishu's new cousins-in-law joked, 'get that one.'

'Isn't she strong?' the women of the majhi's house said to one another when they saw the well-built Rupali heave a sack of paddy on to her shoulder.

'Look, baahu,' they said to her. 'You remind us of your mother-in-law when she was younger. You know, she gave birth to your elder brother-in-law in the middle of that field.'

Over time, she was shown everything. The place where her elder brother-in-law was born, the place where her father-in-law went to work, the place from where her mother-in-law had run like a madwoman, the place where her aunt-in-law practised her special skills. Curious women of the village wondered about the sort of stuff Rupi's second daughter-in-law was made of. Any other woman, they said, would have run away in fright.

Rupali decided she needed more rooms. She discussed this with Bishu.

'More rooms? Inside the house? That's difficult,' he said.

'Then we'll build them outside the house.'

Bishu gazed at her in admiration. The very next morning, they chose a spot in a field some ten metres away from the main house.

Dulari beat her chest. 'The new bride wants to break our house,' she wailed. 'Which chhinar-maiju has taught her all these things?'

Rupali looked her aunt-in-law in the eye. 'No one has taught me anything, kaaki,' she said. 'This is common sense. There is no space in this house for new brides. Where do you expect them to give birth to their babies and bring them up? Dumni-dai is spending her life in a corner. Do you expect me and my children to do the same? What about Phuchu's bride? And what about Saagen's bride, kaaki? Will you deny her the right to live in a bigger space?'

Rupi was impressed. 'Well said, baahu,' she exclaimed, 'very well said. You go build your house.'

The two-room hut was built in a little over two weeks. It was creatively done, and was airy and spacious. Rupali supervised the building of each wall and each corner. There was a broad veranda outside, hemmed by a lattice of bamboo slats. A corner of this veranda was turned into a kitchen. The roof was covered with hay and then covered with taali. On one corner of the roof, a technician from the DTH shop in Chakuliya fixed the disc antenna. Each evening, during the kaalsandhya, Rupali, like diku women, washed her hands and feet, sprinkled some water over her head and lit dhup-batti whose fragrance wafted through the hut and even reached the main house.

Inside this hut, Rupali gave birth to a son and vowed to have no more. The child played with Jaipal's son and Bishu would, in a few years, get them enrolled in a school at his wife's behest.

'These children will spoil everything,' Dulari screamed when the boys ran into her garden. She had aged and lost most of her flab. She had almost become the Dulari of old, when she had come to Kadamdihi as Doso's keep. Her buck teeth weren't fearsome any more.

Dumni hurriedly took her son away. Rupali, however, gave her aunt-in-law an earful. 'They are children, kaaki,' she said, 'not cows or goats that you should drive them away like this. They are playing in your garden, not nibbling at your vegetables.'

'Well said, baahu, well said,' Rupi exclaimed.

Rupi felt healthy enough to hobble into the kitchen and serve Sido his meals. Over time he had become a contented man. He was quite happy to wash and polish his motorcycle with his grandsons, even though he never did learn to ride it, and to cycle all the way to Chakuliya to meet Gurubari. Jaipal, too, had simmered down. It could be that his altercation with Rupi, which had left her unconscious, had scared him. Or perhaps fatherhood had changed him.

Somehow, everything had settled down, and not just the lives of Bishu and Rupali or Jaipal and Dumni. Rupi's health improved, though it seemed unlikely that she would ever regain her full strength. But satisfaction showed on her face and, at times, peace. Putki's drinking did not get better nor did her habit of being indiscreet about the family. But those habits did not bother Rupi anymore. Dulari, of course, did not ascend any teenage girl again, and she had no more confrontations with Rupi.

Rupi marvelled at the changes in her life and curled up to sleep. She slipped into a dream.

She enters the house through the front door. Everything is like before. Sido smiles at her, as does Doso. Khorda-haram sits in one corner of the racha, sipping tea from a tall steel glass, blowing on the tea to cool it. Putki is immaculately dressed, her shrivelled body neatly draped in a light green cotton sari with a purple border, her breasts packed tight within a matching blouse.

'Come, baahu,' she calls out to Rupi to follow her.

Putki leads Rupi behind the house, to the dogor tree. A cool breeze fans her face. Before her stands a two-room hut with bamboo latticework in the veranda. A woman hangs out clothes to dry on a line tied outside the house. A little boy plays in the yard, close to the woman.

'Bishu's wife?' Rupi asks.

'Yes,' Putki replies in her thin, quivering voice. 'And his son.'

Rupi smiles, her face peaceful, her body free of suffering, and lies on the parkom under the dogor tree thinking: Just like me, just like me.

Acknowledgements

The Mysterious Ailment of Rupi Baskey takes cues from an incident which took place in my village and is a creation of village gossip and my imagination.

Sumana Roy monitored my progress and had a word of encouragement at each step. She was the first reader of *The Mysterious Ailment of Rupi Baskey* and became my literary clairvoyant when she said, 'Send it to David Davidar. He has a *very* keen eye. I am pretty sure he will take it on. Try.' I tried. And see!

Besides discussing Shahjahanabad and Delhi, Bollywood—both classic and contemporary—sarkaari naukri and more, Madhulika Liddle gave me the very vital second opinion.

After reading the manuscript, Meru Gokhale asked me a number of questions via email: about me and my job, about Santhals, about Rupi Baskey. Finally, her phone call and a text message from London convinced me that my raw manuscript had some merit.

I can't describe how thrilled I was when I received Ravi Singh's email telling me: 'We'd like very much to publish it in Aleph.' Ravi chose me, and ended up giving me my very own ailment: insomnia.

In my editor, Anurag Basnet, I found a friend and kindred spirit. Over our conversations, I have realized that we share a lot in common, and not just a history of troubled homelands. Anurag's therapy and editorial montro turned Rupi Baskey's story from an 'insulated fable' into a proper novel. He scraped out ideas and memories from the back of my head in the way one scrapes the inside of a coconut to make naarkel-laadoo and in some cases, he gave the flesh and skin of his words to the skeleton of my thoughts and ideas.

Aienla Ozukum, Bena Sareen, David Davidar, Hina Mobar, Meenakshi Singh, Simar Puneet, Sudeshna Shome Ghosh and everyone at Rupa-Aleph daram-dag-ed me wholeheartedly into their very distinguished orak.

The lyrical passage Sido composes, 'Maagh-bonga naase hisid-hisid hoy te', has been sourced from the pamphlet of the gaayaan 'Bidai Bera Re Med-Daak Alom Joro-ya' (Don't Shed Tears at the Hour of Parting), written by Durga Prasad Hembram and produced by the Adim Owar Jarpa Opera, Mayurbhanj, Odisha. All translations are mine.

Marang-Buru aape jhoto ge naay te, naapaay te doho pe maay.

Sahrao ar Johar.

Ghatsila   Hansda Sowvendra Shekhar
27 September 2013